LONELY ROAD MURDER

Rosemary Lennox is horrified to find her best friend and neighbour, Mary Francis, strangled in her flat and it's not long before her husband, John Francis, is also murdered there too. The police question Rosemary, her friend and fellow lodger Bob McDonnell and their landlady Ellen Moreland, but they are unable to establish a motive. However, when Rosemary and Bob attempt to investigate, she discovers that all the evidence points to her friend . . .

JOHN RUSSELL FEARN

---✦---

LONELY ROAD MURDER

Complete and Unabridged

LINFORD
Leicester

First published in Great Britain

First Linford Edition
published 2011

Copyright © 1954 by John Russell Fearn
Copyright © 2011 by Philip Harbottle

British Library CIP Data

Fearn, John Russell, *1908 – 1960.*
  Lonely road murder. - -
  (Linford mystery library)
  1. Murder- -Investigation- -Fiction.
  2. Detective and mystery stories.
  3. Large type books.
  I. Title II. Series
  823.9′12–dc22

ISBN 978–1–44480–646–5

Published by
F. A. Thorpe (Publishing)
Anstey, Leicestershire

Set by Words & Graphics Ltd.
Anstey, Leicestershire
Printed and bound in Great Britain by
T. J. International Ltd., Padstow, Cornwall

1

Gruesome discovery

It was a foggy grey morning. The November air had an icy bite, and the sound of the passing traffic rose in a muffled roar through the open window.

I shut out the disagreeable sight, put the light on, and started to prepare my breakfast. I was very annoyed. All the week, we had basked in wintry sunshine, and now on my day off — fog. Stephen had planned to take me for a drive in the country this afternoon, before our usual Saturday night date, and this beastly weather would stop it. Hopefully I peered again through the curtains, but no, the fog was obviously here to stay.

Perhaps he would phone, he always did if anything went wrong. That was one of the things I liked about him. He was so reliable, you could count on him in any emergency.

Stephen was my boss, at the office, and I had been very flattered and thrilled, when he singled me out. The competition there is unbelievable, we are practically knee-deep in beauties! Saturday was a standing date, and for the last three months he had given me a wonderful time. No one knew that we saw each other outside the office, somehow with a lot of luck we managed to keep our secret from the gossips. It was Mr. Lane and Miss Lennox there but Stephen and Rosemary when we were alone.

The kettle boiling interrupted my reverie, and while I was making the tea, the hall phone with perfect timing began to ring. An ear-splitting yell from the hall nearly made me drop the teapot.

'Rosie! Rosie! Wake up girl. You're wanted on the phone!'

I froze with indignation, and then hurried downstairs.

Bob McDonnell from the top flat, was chatting amiably down the phone, and doodling 'Mrs. Rosie Lane' all over the pad!

I snatched the receiver from him and hissed:

'How dare you shout like that, and if

you call me Rosie any more — '

He grinned. 'Temper! Temper! Don't let old Moneybags hear you.'

Trying to quell Bob is like trying to hold back Niagara with an eggcup. I gave up the attempt, and turned my back on him in a dignified manner.

'Hello Rosemary, Stephen here.'

'Oh, darling, I was hoping you'd ring. We won't be able to go now will we?'

There was a chuckle. 'I'm afraid not, my dear. Still never mind, I've booked a table at Lou's to cheer you up. You love that place, don't you? I'll call at seven. Will that be alright?'

I heaved an ecstatic sigh. 'Oh Stephen, that will be lovely. I was so disappointed before and now I don't mind a bit. Yes seven, darling. Goodbye.'

I mooned happily back up the stairs. Lou's was a heavenly little nightclub. All soft shaded lights. To me it was the most romantic spot I knew, and to crown my happiness, I possessed a new evening gown waiting for just this kind of occasion. I walked into my kitchen glowing with contentment, and then stopped dead. That wretched Bob McDonnell was sitting in the best chair calmly drinking my tea, and reading my paper!

He looked up as I came in, and gave me a sardonic smile. 'Hello, sweet. I've put you out another cup and saucer. Help yourself.'

'You're quite comfortable, I hope?' I said with laboured politeness. 'Wouldn't like an egg or something?'

'No thanks. I'm not hungry. I'll have some toast though. Don't you ever have anything but tea and toast? That's all I ever seem to find round here. Trying to keep your figure, I suppose.'

I breathed fire and fury at this remark, but I kept my temper, which is rather a difficult feat, when Nature has landed you with red hair, green eyes and a temperament to match. Bob stretched out his long legs and put down the paper. I eyed him covertly. He was looking exceptionally smart this morning. The unruly black hair that generally defied his effort was smoothed crisply back. He wore a grey suit and a slightly unconventional pink shirt, which on anyone else would have looked common.

Altogether he was quite presentable.

He caught my glance and laughed. 'Don't look like that my pet. I'm going in a minute. Got to see Mr. Osborne about my novel.'

'He's not accepted?' I cried.

Bob made a magnificent gesture. 'Not definitely, but the man knows talent when he sees it!'

I clapped my hands gleefully. Bob's novel was widely known and believed in, throughout our little block of flats. Its progress from publisher to publisher had been watched with anxious eyes, and this was the first time he had met with anything like encouragement.

I forgot how much he infuriated me and rejoiced for him. His eyes were exultant, but his voice betrayed no excitement as he said casually: 'The interview's at eleven so I'd better be on my way. Wish me luck!'

'Of course I do, Bob.'

He straightened his tie, and brushing off a few toast crumbs walked over to the door. 'Goodbye Rosie.' He paused, frowning slightly. 'By the way does Old Moneybags know that you entertain gentlemen to breakfast in your dressing gown?'

I blushed and pulled it closer round me. 'Must you, Bob? And please don't call Stephen 'Old Moneybags'. It's most rude. He's a charming well educated man, not like that vulgar blonde you've been running around with for the last month!'

He raised a mocking eyebrow. 'Now darling, don't be catty, Stephen thinks she's very nice. He told me so this morning.'

'Oh you — !' I gasped furiously and my temper going fast, I grabbed the tea cosy and threw it. He dodged of course and making a final rude comment at my aim slammed the door. I could hear him laughing as he ran down the stairs. It took me quite a while to simmer down, it generally does after Bob and I have had a little discussion.

I tidied up the flat and by eleven thirty was dressed and ready to go out shopping. I knocked next door to see if

Elly wanted anything. She answered the door, wiping floury hands on her apron. 'Hello dear, just off to the shops?'

'Yes, Elly. Do you want anything?'

'Well, there is something if you're sure it's no bother. I'm right out of gravy salt. Better get me a large packet.'

A heavenly smell was wafting round my nostrils. Elly is a marvellous cook, and her kitchen always sends forth enticing odours.

She smiled at me, her plump rosy face crinkling pleasantly. 'I'm making a rabbit pie. Why don't you come back and have your lunch with me? It'll be ready by one o'clock and there's far too much for me to eat on my own.'

I tried to resist. I'm always eating at Elly's, but she wouldn't hear of it, and laughingly pushing me out of the door told me I was expected at one, and not any later.

Elly had mothered me since the day I moved in. She was such a comfortable person, and I often thought what a loss the male sex had suffered in allowing her to remain unmarried. Plump, kindly, she should have a large family to care for. Not that she ever bothered. Oh no, Elly was far too busy and active. Her life was a happy one.

The fog was really thick, and if I hadn't known my way to the market backwards, I should very soon have been lost. Our 'market' as we call it, was originally a select little backwater, comprising about a dozen small shops. But a few enterprising people pitched their stall there and gradually the idea had taken on, until the shops were outnumbered and the cheeky cockney reigned supreme.

Boxes of tangerines and packets of sticky figs spiked with holly gave a Christmassy air to the fruit stalls, and the fat chickens and slabs of sausage stuffing made me feel quite reckless. I wandered from stall to stall and was just trying to tell myself that the highly priced mushrooms were an unnecessary luxury, when a voice said, 'I should have them, Rosemary — you know you can't resist much longer!'

I turned round in surprise and then laughed as I saw who it was. 'Get thee behind me Satan!'

Mary smiled. 'Well, I'm having some anyway. John adores them.'

We ended up by both buying mushrooms and walked back home together.

Mary was rather quiet as we strolled along. I thought she might be tired and didn't push the conversation. She and her husband John worked in a small nightclub just off Bemers Street. They were the vocalists with Les Roberts' Band, and I envied them their Bohemian life, and late hours. But as if to dispute my thoughts Mary gave a large yawn and said wearily, 'I'm going to spend the rest of the day in bed. This eternal night life is getting me down.'

I wouldn't have this. 'Only the other day you were saying how much you loved it all,' I accused.

She smiled. Mary has a very sweet smile, slanting and sort of pixie-like. 'I do really. Just that I'm a bit fed up. John and I had a row when he got back this morning, and now he's gone off somewhere in a huff.'

I made sympathetic noises and said. 'I

shouldn't worry Mary, he always comes back with a bunch of roses.'

She laughed outright. 'Well, let's hope so. It's all so silly. He keeps getting jealous of Les Roberts and accusing me of being too friendly. What can I do? Les is our boss and if he's nice to me, I can't very well be rude to him. Anyway, he's an awful pet and I like him.'

'Don't let John hear you say that,' I chuckled.

She tossed back the long ash blonde hair that fell in a gleaming sweep to her shoulders. 'Perhaps it would do him good. Oh, that man of mine. I only hope these mushrooms melt his hard heart.'

We had reached the flats by now and after a few more words Mary opened her front door and bade me goodbye.

I glanced at my watch. Yes, it was just on one, Elly would be expecting me.

She was ready and waiting. The table was laid with gleaming silver, and a comforting glow was coming from the fire. 'Did you find your way dear? It's a terrible day. I was surprised at you going out. I know how nervous you are in a fog.'

10

'Oh, it's only at night that I really hate it. There's something rather thrilling about the foggy London street by day.'

Elly shook her head at me. 'Romancing again! Come on now, sit down to your dinner, it'll do you more good than all that silly talk.'

It was a beautiful meal. We finished up with large cups of Elly's special coffee and took them over by the fire to complete the enjoyment. Once settled in the two easy chairs we got down to what Bob rudely calls a 'mothers meeting.' I told Elly all about Stephen, and my new dress and the nightclub we were going to. She was very impressed. Stephen had met her a couple of times, and Elly took to him on sight and loved to hear all the little details of our outings. He was, she informed me, very like an old beau of hers who unfortunately died early in life.

'Oh, I saw Mary Francis this morning,' I said. 'I meant to tell you before.'

'I've not set eyes on her for three days,' Elly declared. 'How is she?'

When I finished the brief story of Mary's troubles, she shook her head and said pityingly, 'Poor thing. I'm sure he hasn't come in yet. I'd have heard him. Perhaps she's sitting there all alone crying.'

'Well, she didn't look much like it when I left her,' I said rather cold-heartedly.

'Now that's thoughtless,' Elly reproved. 'How do you know what was in her mind?'

I shrugged the question aside feeling slightly guilty, and the conversation turned to other things.

It was nearly five before I left but I still had two whole hours to beautify myself. I lazed in my bath delighting in the warm scented water, and the luxury of apparently limitless time. If only life could be as easy and simple all the week through and not just a Saturday wonder!

When I was finally dressed and ready I opened the wardrobe door and surveyed myself with a critical eye in the full-length mirror. The result was surprising. For weeks the dress had tempted me, and now I was thankful that I'd given in and bought it. It was a tawny gold lace shading into leaf brown. The sort of dress that other people seem to have, the sort you never find yourself. I twirled happily and watched the shaded skirt billow and flounce. In happy confidence I waited for Stephen's ring.

★ ★ ★

He was on time. Tall, handsome, everything I admired in a man. As he took me in his arms, and bent his fair head to kiss me, I felt a wave of happiness and excitement run through me at the thought of the evening ahead.

We had a little difficulty in getting to Lou's. The fog, though clearer, was still thick enough to slow the traffic down to a crawl, and our taxi seemed to take ages. However once safely arrived, everything went like a charm. The headwaiter, by good fortune, remembered Stephen, and took us to our table, beautifully placed; near for the floor show, and yet reasonably excluded. Stephen himself was very attentive, and scarcely took his eyes off me throughout the meal. He ordered a special wine, and I drank a lot of it. There was music and laughter everywhere, and I was so happy, I could have danced all alone in the centre of the floor.

Stephen whispered foolish things in my ear as we moved round slowly to the band and held me tightly, and I felt his lips brush against my hair. Oh, it was a wonderful evening. When the music stopped we went reluctantly back to our table. My glass was empty and the waiter brought along another bottle. Stephen raised his glass and toasted me as his 'lovely bewitching Rosemary' and I sat in a dreamy haze.

He was talking, very seriously, and gradually his words began to penetrate . . .

'My Mother naturally wants to meet you.'

His Mother! This brought me down to earth with a definite jolt, and I gave him my full attention.

'I've told her so much about you. She'd like you to come down for a weekend very soon. You'll love her darling. She's a wonderful old lady.'

I was really sitting up and taking notice now. Stephen's mother was the talk of the office. Not that I'd ever paid much attention to gossip, but the old adage 'where there's smoke there's fire' has an uncanny knack of being true, and there was an awful lot of smoke around Stephen's mother. Only last week, Sandra, our typist had declared: 'He's properly tied to his Mummy's apron strings. That old lady rules the roost. I'll bet she'll pick his wife for him personally, and then tell him to go ahead and propose.'

At the time I'd laughed and asked where she got her information, but now thinking back, I wasn't laughing.

Obviously a visit to Stephen's home was tantamount to a proposal. There was nothing I wanted more, but, supposing I didn't come up to his mother's standards?

I gazed at Stephen aghast. He apparently saw no change in me, and continued. 'How about next week, darling? Will that suit you?'

'That would be lovely,' I stammered, but my voice was not exactly enthusiastic; and I was thankful when the subject dropped.

Somehow after that, the stardust was gone from the evening, and the wine made me feel hot and flushed, not exhilarated. Quite a lot of people were leaving. It was barely eleven, and I remarked on it to Stephen.

'The fog I expect,' he answered and began to look worried.

The fog! I'd completely forgotten the weather, but as more and more people began to get up and go, I grew a little apprehensive. 'Perhaps we ought to leave now Stephen,' I said with an anxious glance. 'It must have got thicker.'

He was quite agreeable, and while he attended to the cheque, I hurried into the cloakroom. All chaos was let loose there. An elderly woman in a mink coat cried hysterically that the traffic had come to a standstill and she knew it was the end of the world. A slinky brunette was bewailing her fate and saying there was nothing for it but the underground and her shoes would be ruined. Others were searching for torches and in one corner about half a dozen battled for possession of the phone. I got my coat and bag as quickly as possible and left them to it. Stephen was waiting. 'Come on darling, we'll have to go home by tube, and we'd better hurry,

16

there'll be a terrible crush.'

Out in the street, the fog had closed right in, enveloping everything in a thick impenetrable gloom. We could scarcely see a hand in front of us, but after a lot of false starts and bumping into people, we managed to reach the station.

The platform was crowded, and I tried vainly to keep my skirt away from all the shuffling feet but someone caught their heel in it and I heard a horrible rending noise. This, on top of everything else, nearly reduced me to tears, and when Stephen hesitantly suggested that he should stay on the train (it was a direct line for him) when I got off, I could have wept in earnest.

A little sober thought soon made me realize how foolish I was being. My flat was just round the comer from the station, and I knew the way blindfolded. Of course once I agreed to his suggestion Stephen began to worry and say that he would come with me; but I settled the question by patting his hand, whispering: 'See you Monday, darling,' and slipped quickly through the doors when we arrived at Baker Street, before he could follow me.

He waved frantically from behind the closing doors. I blew him a kiss, and gathering my skirts, made for the escalator. Once arrived at the top, a new mishap awaited me. I realized the purpose of Stephen's frantic gestures — he still held my ticket! By the time I had explained my plight to the collector, and paid my fare for the distance the little crowd of people who had come up with me had melted away, and a curious sense of isolation seemed to invade the station.

I gave myself a mental shake to dispel this silly idea, and walked firmly out of the station. Barely two steps further the lighted entrance was a blurred dim shape, and the inky blackness surrounded me completely. There was no sound but my own startlingly loud steps as I hurried along, one hand feeling the wall. I wished now that I had let Stephen come with me. Though I knew my way so well I was already hesitating and a lamppost looming suddenly up in front brought me to an abrupt halt.

I stood perfectly still, trying to get my bearings — my heart thudding. The only lamppost on this road was at the corner of Chaplin Street: that meant I was barely fifty yards from home. I ran that fifty yards stumbling and half sobbing in a blind panic. I am not really a nervous person, but the fog had sent my bravery to the four winds, and the fear of a hand suddenly touching me, or a face leering over my shoulder was too much — I ran!

I pushed through the swing door of the flats with a sense of blessed relief and leant breathless and shaken against the wall. Even here the fog had penetrated and the usually bright warm hall was misty and chill. A gathering menace seemed to hang in the air.

I crossed the hall towards the staircase telling myself not to be so hysterical. I had one foot on the first stair, when I noticed the door of John and Mary's flat was open. Perplexed, I halted. That was funny. They were always so careful about locking up, more so than the rest of us, as they were on the ground floor. It was nearly twelve. That meant they wouldn't be home for a couple of hours yet, maybe later as the traffic wasn't running. The best thing would be to shut it anyway.

I turned back, and paused again. I could see through to their bedroom, and from under the bedroom door came a thin thread of light. Yes, and faintly I heard the radio playing.

'Anyone at home?' I called softly. There was no answer. I called again, louder this time. There was still no reply. Puzzled, I pushed the door open and going in knocked rather hesitantly on their bedroom door. There was still no answer, only the music was louder now.

Suddenly I was afraid.

With trembling fingers I turned the handle and thrust back the door. There, huddled on the floor, face contorted, eyes fixed and staring, lay the body of Mary Francis.

2

Inspector Nevil's suspicions

Sheer terror gripped me by the throat as I stared at Mary's huddled pitiful body. I tried to scream, to run from that horror-filled room, but my legs refused to move.

The sudden jarring note of the hall clock as it struck the hour seemed to release me, and I screamed. Screamed and screamed — turning to half run, half stumble towards the door. The sound of voices and people hurrying down the stairs were mingling now with my cries. I heard a man shout: 'It's coming from here!' and Bob McDonnell burst into the room.

I flung myself on him screaming and sobbing in wild hysteria, clutching frantically at his coat. Words poured from me. 'Mary's been strangled! She's been murdered! The door was open and I came in and found her. Oh, Bob! Bob!'

He gave one startled horrified glance over my shoulder, and putting his arms about me held me tightly. 'There, darling. You're all right now, I'm here, I won't let anything happen to you. Don't cry so. There's nothing to be afraid of.'

Elly's motherly figure robed in an old fashioned blue dressing gown, detached itself from the little crowd that had gathered in the doorway and Bob turned to her saying in a relieved gasp: 'Oh, Elly. Thank God you're here. Take Rosemary back to your room. She's in a terrible state. I'll be up later. We'll have to get on to the police.' He locked the bedroom door. Elly shepherded me through the excited crowd, indignantly returning the stares we received.

Once safely in her room, she put me gently into an armchair and hustled about, putting on the kettle and turning on the electric fire. I was very cold, my teeth were chattering and the tears ran down my cheeks, She glanced at me anxiously, and abandoning her tasks, sat down beside me, chafing my icy, shivering body.

'My poor baby,' she crooned. 'What a terrible thing for you to see. Try not to think about it.'

'But who would want to kill Mary?' I sobbed. 'Everybody liked her. It's terrible, like some ghastly nightmare. John will be crazy with grief. Poor John, poor Mary.'

Elly did her best to calm me, but I could see that she was as shocked and horrified as I was. Her capable hands were trembling as she poured me out a cup of tea. 'Now drink this up, Rosemary,' she begged. 'It'll do you good.'

Obediently I sipped the hot sweet tea, and it did seem to help a little. The fire was glowing hotly now and in the comfort and reassurance of simple ordinary things I began to grow calmer.

There was a great deal of noise downstairs and we found ourselves talking in low fearful tones while we listened. Suddenly there was a knock at the door. Elly adjusted her dressing gown. 'That'll be Bob.' It was, but not alone. Towering behind him was a policeman, accompanied by a middle aged grey-haired man, with a queer bird-like appearance. Bob patted my shoulder and said gently, 'Feeling a bit better, Rosemary?'

I nodded.

The little birdman came over to me, a notebook in hand. 'You are the Miss Lennox who found the body?' he stated in a matter of fact way. 'My name is Nevil. Inspector Nevil. I'm afraid we have an unpleasant task ahead of us. If you will be good enough to tell me exactly what happened, we'll get it over as soon as possible. At what time did you make the discovery?'

'About twelve,' I answered nervously. 'I remember glancing at the clock as I came in.'

'Mmm. What happened then?'

'I crossed the hall and was just going upstairs when I noticed Mary's door was open. I thought it strange as they are always so careful about locking up.' I paused.

'Yes — ' he encouraged.

'Well, I went in and saw that there was a light showing under the bedroom door, and I could hear the radio playing. I

24

called, but nobody answered, so I walked through and opened the door, and saw her lying — ' I broke off, my mouth stiff and dry as the recollection of that moment swept over me.

Elly shifted in her chair and flared angrily. 'Is all this necessary, Inspector? You can see she's in no fit state for questioning.'

He cleared his throat and gave her a reproachful look. 'My dear lady, we have our job to do. It's unpleasant I know, but these things must be gone into if we are to get a clear picture of what occurred.' Turning to Bob he continued smoothly, 'The husband, you say, is on his way here?'

Bob nodded. 'I got through to him at the club where they work. Poor devil. I didn't know how to break it to him. They worshipped each other.'

'You say 'they'; did Mrs. Francis work with him?'

'Yes. They're the vocalists with Les Roberts' band.'

'Why was she not there tonight?'

Bob hesitated as he realized the

frightening implications behind his next words. 'I believe they had quarrelled.'

Inspector Nevil raised his eyebrows and exchanged a brief glance with the constable, who was busily taking down the conversation. 'Indeed!'

'There's nothing in that,' Elly broke in quickly. 'Young people often have little tiffs.'

'Quite so, quite so,' he agreed imperturbably.

A sudden knock at the door startled us. The constable opened it. John Francis stood there, his face white and drawn, his eyes hard. 'My wife!' he choked. 'They won't let me see her. There's a policeman on the door and I can't get in. Where is she? What have you done to her?'

Inspector Nevil gripped his arm in a kindly way. 'I'm very sorry, Mr. Francis,' he said gently. 'If you'll come downstairs with me.' He led the way accompanied by the large constable, and left us alone.

Bob sat down with a sigh. 'Any more tea going, Elly? I could do with something.'

'Of course, dear.' She bustled into the

kitchen, and Bob lit two cigarettes, handing one over to me. We sat in silence until the Inspector came back.

The constable was half supporting John, who leaned on him heavily, like a drunken man. They put him in a chair and made him drink the fresh tea Elly brought in, while Bob hovered protectively behind. My heart ached for him and I turned away to hide the tears. The Inspector stood by quietly. After a bit he expressed his sympathy, and made the same remarks about having to ask questions. I clenched my hands tightly and waited.

'Do you know of anyone who had reason to kill your wife, Mr. Francis?'

John gazed at him blankly. 'Kill Mary? No, I can't think of anyone.'

'You say some of her jewellery and a lace housecoat are missing?'

John nodded. This was news to me. 'It must have been burglars then!' I cried.

Inspector Nevil ignored my interruption. 'At what time did you last see your wife?'

'About a quarter past seven. We had an argument, and I spent the afternoon over at some friends. I came back to change for the club. Mary was already dressed, but one thing led to another and we quarrelled again. She said I could go alone, that she didn't care if she never saw me again — ' The harsh voice cracked and burying his head in his hands, he sobbed like a child. 'My lovely, lovely Mary!' He got to his feet and stood swaying and sobbing. Elly darted forward with a warning cry, and just in time Bob caught him as he fell.

They soon brought him to, and I saw the horror and misery creep back into his dazed eyes. The policeman said expertly, 'He'll be alright after this. The shock often takes them that way,' and the questions began again.

The time of death had been established between seven and eight. Bob spent the evening at a party, he had left the building at seven thirty and returned at about a quarter to twelve. Mary's door he asserted had been closed. Elly had left for the cinema at six thirty and got home at eleven, after having supper with her niece. She too insisted that the door was shut.

Stephen had picked me up at seven and the rest of course they knew.

'Got that all down, Johnson?'

'Yes sir.'

Inspector Nevil regarded us thoughtfully. 'It's strange about that door, perhaps it was not fastened securely and clicked open. I'm not quite satisfied on that point. Perhaps it will clear itself up. We'll need to take a few more statements and check these alibis.' He turned to John and we held our breath. 'Your story Mr. Francis puts you in a very difficult position. We know that your wife died not later than eight o'clock. On your own telling you were with her until about seven thirty and apparently the last to see her alive. I'm afraid you'll have to come down to the station and make a statement. Purely a matter of form, of course.'

John got up. He looked very old in that moment, but his voice was steady as he replied. 'I did not kill my wife, Sir. I know everything seems to point that way, but I did not kill her. My conscience is clear.'

'In that case there can be no objection to your accompanying us.' The Inspector continued smoothly, 'The rest of you can carry on normally. I regret the trouble you have been put to. You understand, of course, that none of you can leave the district without notifying the police. He motioned John in a kindly way to the door.

Bob said quickly, 'How long will it take, Sir?'

'The statement? An hour, maybe not that.'

'Well, if I have your permission Inspector, I'll come along and wait for Mr. Francis.'

The Inspector looked at him quizzically. 'Very well.'

There was a pause while Bob ran upstairs for his coat, and then the little procession started down the stairs.

Left alone, Elly and I sat gazing unhappily at each other. I moistened my lips. 'They think John did it, don't they?'

She nodded. 'It certainly seems that way. Taking him down to the police station as if he were a criminal — why, he's nearly off his head with the shock of it.'

I leaned back in my chair. 'I can't believe it's happened, Elly. Everything seems too unreal. Poor John.'

'If they'd only use some sense,' Elly said, angrily, gathering up the cups and banging them on the tray. 'Her jewels are missing and they won't even talk about robbery.' She stalked into the kitchen and I got up wearily.

'My bed's all ready, dear,' she called. 'You can't possibly sleep on your own tonight. No child, I won't hear of it. There's plenty of room for two.'

I made very little objection to her kind offer, and crept thankfully into bed beside her, wearing a voluminous old fashioned nightdress that she insisted on lending me, and fell almost at once into a deep dreamless sleep.

* * *

I slept very late. When I woke, I couldn't imagine where I was, or what I was doing in that ridiculous nightdress. Slowly at first, and then with a horrid swiftness, all the nightmare returned. I got up, and swathing myself in a blue dressing gown I found lying across the foot of the bed I went into the kitchen. There was no sign of Elly, so I gathered my clothes and bag and quietly let myself into my own flat.

I bathed and dressed, then made some breakfast. I didn't feel very much like eating though, I thought how yesterday Bob had laughed at my tea and toast hospitality, I thought of Mary's slanting smile and her gay voice urging me to buy the mushrooms. Yesterday had been so full of laughter and good things, and now we were caught up in a different world. There was little to laugh at today.

Somebody knocked at the door, and I jumped nervously. 'It's me,' Elly called. She came in busting with news. 'John's home. So everything must be alright. I saw him on the stairs just now. He slept the night at Bob's. I didn't like to ask him any questions, poor thing — he still seems sort of numbed. Those policemen are checking our alibis, too. I had a phone call from my niece this morning, asking me what I'd been up to — and — look at the papers!

Pausing for breath she handed me the morning, papers, and I gasped. Headlines leapt out.

'Girl strangled in flat'.

'Husband questioned'.

'Nightclub singer found murdered'.

Shuddering I put them down. Elly nodded shrewdly.

'There's a young feller down in the hall asking all sorts of questions. Says he's a reporter from the *Daily Sun*,' she said indignantly. 'He wanted to see you, but I soon sent him packing.'

Fascinated against my will, I read the lurid accounts. They had it all in, detail for detail. How many murder accounts I must have read without bothering about the feelings of those involved, and how different it seemed touching one's own life.

Elly flopped down into the armchair. 'Thank the Lord it's Sunday,' she said piously. 'I couldn't have faced Mrs. Samuel's today.' Mrs. Samuels was an elderly lady whom Elly visited about three times each week. I don't quite know what her duties consisted of, mostly compan- ionship I believe, but from all accounts the lady was something of a tartar. I often wondered why she stood for it. It wasn't the money, because Elly had a small annuity, and was quite comfortable financially.

Thinking of Elly's toiling, reminded me of my own. 'I hope there won't be a lot of talk in the office,' I said apprehensively.

'Bound to be,' she returned dryly. 'People are always inquisitive.'

I nearly smiled at this, considering Elly's appreciation of a juicy scandal. 'I wonder what the police are doing? I'm sure they think John killed her, although they haven't arrested him.'

'Poor John,' Elly cried passionately. 'If that Inspector Nevil had kept on much longer last night, I think he would have been driven out of his mind.'

'Is the room still locked?' I asked.

'No. The constable on duty said he'd be going this afternoon. They've seen all they want now. I suppose John will stay with friends though. He could hardly live here now.'

I sighed at that. The terror that had struck last night would leave its mark on more than one.

A little while later Bob came in. He looked tired and dispirited. He answered our questions and then fell silent. I glanced at my watch. Barely two o'clock and all the rest of the day stretching endlessly ahead. Elly seemed to sense my mood as I shifted restlessly in my chair. She got up briskly and fixed us with a determined eye. 'Well, if we sit around here mooning all week, it won't change anything. I think I'll pop over to my niece's, she wanted me to. Why don't you two go out? Have a meal and pay the cinema a visit? It will do you good and take your mind off things.'

Bob nodded thoughtfully and looked across at me. 'She's right, you know. We must do something. How about it, Rosemary?'

I accepted the offer thankfully, feeling only too glad of the opportunity; and after a quick rush round we all left the flats together.

There was no trace of yesterday's fog. The sky was bright and clear, with an occasional burst of sunshine. There were quite a number of people about; all walking rapidly, and talking of their own affairs, and it was impossible not to fall in with the normality of life.

We decided on the little restaurant round the corner, and in the bustle of finding seats and ordering the meal, we were at last able to relax. I found to my surprise that I was quite hungry, and when Bob said: 'What will you have for a sweet, Rosie?' I consulted the menu with a genuine interest.

As the waitress went away he laughed across at me. 'That's better, my pet. You're beginning to look like my favourite redhead again. Mavellous what a little food will do. It's all that tea and toast you live on, bound to get you a down a bit in the end!'

'Bob, you are an old darling. You can always make me see something to laugh at.'

He grinned. 'Well, you'll smile in a different way tomorrow, when you see what plum pudding and custard has done for your figure. Stephen will be sending me complaints.'

'Stephen!'

'Poor Old Moneybags,' Bob sighed addressing the menu with a long face. 'She's forgotten all about you — Never given you a thought all day!'

I felt extremely guilty! Bob was quite correct. I had not given Stephen a moment's thought throughout the day. All this horrible business had driven him completely from my mind. 'Do you think he'll see it in the papers?' I asked anxiously.

'Of course he will. Right bang on the front page. Mother won't like it a bit either, probably think her darling boy's caught up with a terrible creature!'

Now this was a little too good a guess to be comfortable. Bob's inane chatter was perhaps very much to the point

Stephen's mother would definitely not feel kindly disposed towards her son's future wife if she had had her name in all the papers as a murder witness. I sighed despondently.

'Cheer up,' said Bob cheerfully as the waitress brought our plum puddings. 'She'll forgive you. Let's eat this and then we can find out what's on at the cinema. I'll treat you.'

'That's very handsome,' I replied, sarcasm getting the better of my natural feminine sweetness.

'No, don't thank me,' he implored. 'Mr. Osborne says I show great promise, so I'll find the money this once.'

'Your book! Your beautiful book! He's accepted it!'

'Not yet. But he's having another think about it.'

'I know he'll take it,' I beamed. 'You'll be as rich as Croesus.'

'Not on one novel, darling, and he hasn't accepted it yet. I wish you wouldn't put out the flags so quickly. I'll tell you when to start cheering.'

'I can't help it. I'm so excited for you.'

'Well, forget it for a bit, and do hurry. I shall have to spend half the profits I haven't made yet, on buying expensive seats.'

I hastily began to eat my pudding. Really, how Bob's girl friends stuck to him through this kind of treatment was beyond me. They must be made of iron to stand it, unless of course, love has a softening influence on him.

After a lot of arguing we decided on the Ritz Plaza, and an American comedy. It was a good film, and we laughed a lot.

I was quite sorry to come out. Bob consulted his watch. 'It's only seven, Rosie. Let's go into Charlie's.' At any other time I would have refused indignantly, but tonight was different, so to Charlie's we went.

Charlie's is a little pub, squeezed between two very old and derelict offices. It's one and only claim to charm is that you seldom meet the same people there twice, and that is a trait not to be sniffed at. It was fairly quiet, and after a few words with the proprietor, whose name you can probably guess. Bob bought a plate of sandwiches, a pint of beer and a gin and orange and we esconced ourselves at a little table in the corner.

I sipped my drink, idly looking around me.

'Got any cigarettes, Rosie? I'm clean out.'

'Here you are,' I said. 'I've got plenty. Do you want any for later on?'

Bob carefully pocketed half the contents of my case and flicked irritably at the lighter. 'It doesn't work,' I informed him needlessly.

'Indeed it doesn't,' he muttered. 'Here.'

He lit our cigarettes and tossed me over the box of matches.

'Better keep it. I've got another.'

I slipped the matches into my pocket and then gave a violent start as a voice suddenly hissed in my ears. 'I read it all in the papers, Miss. A dreadful shaking you must have had.' It was Charlie! Seizing his opportunity while it was a bit quiet, he had come over for 'a bit of talk' as he expressed it. John and Mary had often dropped in here, and he knew them well. There was genuine sympathy in his eyes and we could not resent his well-meant enquiries.

I told him the facts as briefly as I could. I managed to keep my voice level but towards the end of the story a little tremble crept in despite my efforts.

Charlie heard me out, and then turned to Bob. 'He never done it,' he said simply. 'Young Mr. Francis worshipped the ground his pretty little Mrs. walked on. No, it was robbery, if you ask me.'

'That's what I told the Inspector,' I responded eagerly. 'Didn't I Bob?'

He nodded agreement. 'I'd stake my

life on John. He isn't the type. Someone somewhere holds the key to it all.'

I shivered. There was a horrible certainty in Bob's voice that sent a chill through me — It was true, but I hadn't thought of it that way before. In all the teeming crowds someone was sitting talking. Just as we were, even laughing perhaps. But beneath it all, locked in his heart was the terrible knowledge of murder: that last night he had choked a woman to death with his bare hands. He might even be here.

'I think I'd like another drink please,' I said hastily.

Charlie raised his hand significantly. 'On the house, this one. I'll send them over. Same as last time?' We thanked him, and he went back, ducking under the counter with the ease of long practice.

Soon after we left, and strolled slowly home. When we reached the flats, I hurried past that silent door now mercifully shut. The hall had ceased to be a warm inviting place to me, loneliness hovered in the air and I was glad of Bob's comforting presence. At the door of my flat I paused, fear still strong in me, and Bob seemed to understand. He leaned back against the wall and smiled kindly.

'Now I'll tell you what we'll do Rosie. It's too early to go in yet. Come upstairs into the spider's parlour, and I'll make you a cup of genuine bachelor coffee!' I accepted gratefully and we went up.

Bob's flat was in a terrible state. The bed still unmade and the couch he had slept on last night while John stayed, tumbled with rugs and pillows. The remains of a hasty breakfast littered the table and the ashtrays overflowed with cigarette ends.

'Pardon any dust that may offend your housewifely eyes,' he offered without a blush.

'Dust!' I cried in horror. 'Never mind the dust. Just look at this mess. I'll tidy up a bit. I couldn't enjoy my coffee with all this clutter around me.' Bob shrugged and ambled into the kitchen.

Left alone I tackled the room vigorously. Bustling around did me good, and by the time I had achieved some sort of order out of that chaos, I felt myself again. Bob meanwhile had finally found two clean cups, and made the coffee. A further search revealed a box of cookies. 'Elly's — you scrounger,' I accused, and we settled by the gas fire companionably enough.

The coffee was surprisingly good. I complimented Bob, who received my remarks with a degree of complacency that nearly made me take them back again; and time went on. It went on so quickly that the clock striking eleven pulled me up with a shock. Bob shook his head significantly over the doubtful morals of young women, who stayed in men's flats till all hours, then grinned and said: 'I enjoyed today. Rosie. It helped didn't it?'

'Oh. Bob. You'll never know how much.'

He laughed. 'Well, if you insist on going. May I escort you home?'

'I think I can manage one flight of stairs on my own Kind Sir! Goodnight, Bob, and thanks for — the coffee.' I waved my hat at him and went softly down to my flat.

It was silly to be scared, surrounded by friends as I was. I undressed, washed and sat down in front of the mirror, to brush my hair, humming under my breath. Relaxed and content, I sat, the rhythm of the brush soothing away my last care, when suddenly I heard a noise — A sort of scratching sound behind me.

I turned round quickly. My bedroom door was open and I could see right through to the living room. The knob on the door was being gently turned. Somebody was trying to get in!

I got up and walked slowly across the room. The turning had stopped and I said nervously: 'Who is it?'

There was no reply. With trembling fingers I released the catch and pulled the door out. The passage was silent and completely deserted!

3

Another death

I slept badly. For a long time I lay awake, my nerves jumping at every little sound. Slowly, very slowly the night wore on. Downstairs in the hall the clock chimed the hours. Twelve, one, two, until round about three o'clock; I fell asleep from sheer exhaustion.

The alarm jangling loudly in my ear woke me after what seemed only a few seconds. I got up thankfully rejoicing in the daylight's return, and pulled back the curtains. The sun was hidden behind the grey clouds, but it was light and that was all I cared.

My fears seemed a little foolish now. I even began to wonder if I had imagined someone trying my door last night. After all, what possible reason could anyone have for attempting to break in? There were no jewels or money to steal in my flat. Reassuring myself thus, I decided not to mention the incident to Elly or Bob. They would only make a fuss, and I should be frightened all over again.

I gulped down my breakfast, and decided to wear my grey jersey for the office. Worn with my double row of pearls, it was very effective, and I wanted to look my best for Stephen. He would be certain to seek me out as soon as I arrived.

No one was about, I couldn't hear any signs of Elly stirring next door, and Bob left for his office half an hour after me. I shut the door quietly, and set out for the bus stop. I bought a paper at the corner, and glancing rapidly through it found a half paragraph on the second page re-listing the details of Mary's death, and adding that the police were confident of an early arrest. Well, that was something anyway. The sooner this terrible business was cleared up and suspicion lifted from John, the better I should like it.

The bus was a long time coming, but I didn't mind. I had no desire to be early at the office. I could imagine what kind of reception awaited me there. I was not mistaken. Hardly had the doors closed behind me than I found myself the centre of an excited crowd of girls all yelling questions. I answered them as best I could. It was understandable really. Had it been any of the others, I should have formed a part of that eager group wanting to hear all about it.

Sandra, our typist, swung her long elegant legs and waved a paper at me. 'I couldn't believe my eyes,' she reiterated for about the tenth time. 'There it was as plain as your hat. 'The body was found by Miss Rosemary Lennox'. Rosemary Lennox? I said to Mum. Why, I work with her! I don't know how I stopped myself from coming right round to you.'

I thanked my lucky stars that she hadn't come, and made some suitable reply. Conversation was at its height. Work was at a standstill, when the buzzer ringing impatiently from Stephen's room galvanized us into action. Reaching for my notebook and pencil I practically ran in.

Stephen was pacing the floor with long agitated steps. At the sight of me he stopped, and pulling me towards him said: 'Oh, my poor darling. What a terrible shock you must have had. I read it all in the papers.' My resistance broke at this and I put my head on his shoulder, and sobbed, forgetting my desire to look attractive. He wiped my eyes tenderly with his big handkerchief, and patted me soothingly. 'I've been nearly demented thinking of you Rosemary. If only I hadn't let you go home on your own none of this would have happened.'

'No,' I answered shakily. 'It was nothing to do with you, darling. Someone would have found Mary anyway. It was all there like a book, waiting for us to open it.'

'I see they've questioned the husband, and let him go. Can't think why, everything points to his guilt.'

'John? He never killed Mary. He worshipped her, Stephen. If you'd seen him that night when they broke the news, you'd know he was innocent.'

He shrugged his shoulders. 'Well, you're closer to it than I am of course, and that may be prejudicing you in his favour. We can none of us see our friends as murderers.'

'He's not a murderer — ' I broke in indignantly.

'No, no, of course he isn't.' Stephen soothed and patted me again.

He moved round to his desk and began sorting through some papers, while I dried my eyes. When I looked up he smiled and said, 'Better? Good. Now, Rosemary, I've been thinking. I don't feel it would be very wise for you to stay at this office. You'll have people talking about this affair all the time, and it will only upset you. Why not take a few days rest?'

'Oh Stephen, do you really think I could? Will you be able to manage?'

He laughed. 'We'll probably stagger along somehow. Off you go.' I kissed his cheek gratefully, a little spark of mischief running through me as he hurriedly wiped the lipstick off and glanced apprehensively at the door. 'I'll phone you tonight, Rosemary. Get some fresh air, you look so pale. Goodbye darling.'

'Goodbye, Mr. Lane,' I said demurely and blowing him a kiss, I left the room.

The girls were very sympathetic.

Sandra's sharp eyes detected the traces of tears on my face and she nodded significantly as I told them I wouldn't be in for a few days. 'Best thing you could do, ducky. Buy yourself a new hat or something. It'll cheer you up and take your mind off things.'

I put my coat on and bade them all goodbye. 'Don't forget to let us know if anyone else gets bumped off,' she yelled as I closed the door, and I couldn't help laughing.

The prospect of all this freedom was very pleasing and I felt quite light-hearted, as I walked along to the bus stop, bound for Oxford Street. I took Sandra's advice and bought a new hat. My intentions had not been to do so, but I was cornered by a persuasive salesgirl, who wouldn't hear of my leaving the shop without one.

The sun was shining brightly and as it was really quite a warm day for November. I determined to lunch in the park. In about half an hour's time I was sitting on an empty bench by the Serpentine, clutching two packets of sandwiches and an apple tart.

Everywhere was bright and cheerful. A group of schoolboys, playing truant, fished patiently for tiddlers. Further up a young couple stood watching the water, engrossed in each other. I settled back feeling at peace with the world, and began to eat my sandwiches. They were very nice and tasted so much better in the open air, but I couldn't help feeling a little conspicuous. I glanced up to see if anyone was watching, half wishing I'd brought a book or something, and in the distance I saw a familiar figure coming towards me. It was John Francis.

As he came nearer I saw how pale and set his face was. He seemed suddenly aged and lonely. My heart melted, and jumping up, heedless of my parcels, I ran across to him and touched his arm. He started and gave me a blank stare, then he smiled vaguely and said, 'Hullo, Rosemary, no work today?'

'No work,' I gulped. 'I'm having my lunch in the park for a change, come over and join me.'

John made no protest and let me lead

him, as if he were a child, back to my seat. I handed him the other packet of sandwiches and watched so that he ate something. He finished them obediently, and sat gazing dully into space. I sought vainly for the right words, frantically I racked my brains for some means of comforting him, but nothing came. I offered a cigarette, but he never noticed.

'I've been trying to think who could have killed her,' he began abruptly, in a harsh, surprisingly loud, voice. 'I've thought and thought, but there's no one, no one.' He turned round suddenly and gripped my wrist. 'Who'd do it Rosemary? Who did this wicked thing to her? They killed me too you know. Oh, I eat and sleep, go through the motions of living, but I'm dead. Dead, do you hear?'

His voice rose and I cast an apprehensive look round saying as calmly as I could. 'You mustn't dwell on it so John. You'll make yourself ill. The police will find the murderer.'

He relaxed the grip on my wrist and said awkwardly. 'Forgive me, Rosemary, I don't know what I'm saying any more.'

He got up. 'I'm going back to the flat. No, don't try to stop me, my dear. I'll be alright. It'll help me to go back. There's a lot of stuff to be cleared up, Mary's things — ' Giving me a smile he walked slowly away.

I watched him pityingly, a lump rising in my throat. To what a home he was going, that poor lonely man.

The sun had disappeared, and the air was no longer warm. I shivered and gathered my parcels together The park had lost its cheerfulness, and I wandered off rather dispiritedly thinking that perhaps I should have stayed at the office. Freedom was all very well, but it gave one too much time to think.

On an impulse I entered a little theatre booking office, and bought a couple of seats for one of the current shows. It was ages since I had taken Elly out and it would cheer her enormously, after all the trouble. I phoned the flats, and at Elly's cheerful 'Miss Moreland here who do you wish to speak to?' eagerly proposed my plans for the evening. She was delighted. 'What time shall I meet you dear?'

'Better make it about seven,' I said. 'I'm going have my hair set this afternoon, if I can fix an appointment. Oh, I saw John in the park. He's terribly upset, said he was going to clear up Mary's things.'

Elly clicked her tongue sympathetically. 'Poor dear, I don't suppose I shall see him though. I promised to get some shopping in for Mrs. Samuels, and I'm just off. Lucky you phoned when you did, or I'd have missed you. I should have been sorry. I'll meet you at Piccadilly then. Yes I remember dear, by that little place where we had tea before.'

She rang off and I fed in more coins and rang my hairdresser's number. Yes they could fit me in if I came at once. I picked up that wretched hat bag, sincerely wishing I had never bought the thing and set off for Madame Gray's. I always have my hair done there, when I can afford it, and the girl who did my hair there was an old friend.

Today however, I never set eyes on her. Madame Gray herself received me, gushing and gracious, her snow-white hair dressed magnificently in an elegant pompadour, her hands waving expressively. I was overwhelmed at such an honour. Madame generally reserved her personal service for her wealthier clientele, not an insignificant shampoo and set like myself. She ushered me into a softly lit cubicle and summoned one of the staff to take my outdoor things. Marvelling, I settled comfortably into the padded chair, but Madame's opening remark speedily dealt a shattering blow at any ideas, I might have been getting on my own importance. 'I see by the newspapers that you are the young lady who found the dead nightclub singer Miss Lennox.'

I reflected ironically that I was becoming quite famous in a small way, and resigned myself to more curiosity

The nauseating questions finally came to an end. Madame fixed the dryer in position and left me to merciful solitude. I was glad when it was over and I could pay up and go.

It was quite early and I had a couple of hours to while away until Elly met me. I spent them in a half empty teashop. No one took the least notice of me, once I was served, and I believe I could have sat there till closing time without disturbing the staff. Indeed the waitress looked quite put out when I interrupted her game of cards with the cashier, to pay my bill.

I arrived at our rendezvous with ten minutes to spare and waited patiently for Elly. This was small matter. Elly had an amazing knack of misunderstanding the simplest instructions and was quite capable of waiting outside the Bank of England, in serene belief that, that was where I told her to be. By some miracle, she did nothing of the sort, and prompt to the minute, her matronly figure appeared triumphantly before me, a large bag of sweets clutched in her hand. 'I thought we'd like a few chocolates to munch,' she informed me, tucking her arm.

It was a very good show. Elly thought it was a little bit suggestive, but that did not prevent her from giggling and laughing, throughout the performance. I had seldom seen her laugh so much, and got more pleasure from watching her reactions, than I did from watching the players, excellent as they were.

We had supper. Elly does so much cooking that I thought it would be a welcome change for her to eat a meal and not have to prepare it first. I ordered a four course meal, and we were halfway through it, when Elly suddenly jumped up and waved her fork urgently at someone. I turned round in some surprise. Coming towards us nodding and smiling was none other than Inspector Nevil!

I was very disconcerted, but Elly who had conceived a violent dislike of the man practically on sight, welcomed him warmly and begged him to join us. He pulled up a chair and sat down. 'Well, well, this is an unexpected meeting ladies,' he said affably. Although he was off-duty I couldn't rid myself of the feeling that he was watching us closely and that at any minute a constable would appear at his elbow to take down our conversation.

'Have you found out anything yet?' Elly queried eagerly. 'We are so anxious to hear if the murderer is discovered.'

He frowned slightly, and I burned to warn her not to press for any information. It was obvious he could not discuss the case. 'You are not more anxious than the police, Miss Moreland. You may be sure that everything possible has been done, is being done, but in the event of an arrest you will be informed through the excellent offices of the press only.' His lips closed firmly and I hastened to change the subject.

'We have just come from the Athenium Theatre Inspector Nevil.'

'Indeed! A pleasant farce, I believe.' Fortunately at that moment the girl arrived to take his order, and I took the opportunity of treading on Elly's toes and shaking my head at her warningly. She smiled reassuringly and as the Inspector turned his attention back to us again, began discussing the lack of taste in restaurant cooked food.

'I've always wondered what they do with it,' she wailed, 'give them a perfectly good piece of lamb and they beat all the nourishment from it and serve it up with watery vegetables. I wish I had the cooking of some of their joints.' She had struck the right chord. Inspector Nevil confessed himself a connoisseur of good food, and under her influence expanded and shone, until he became quite human. I forgot my fear and we sat chatting like three old friends.

I grew a little bored after half an hour of recipes, and fell to recalling my first impressions of him. A little bird-like man I had called him, and that exactly described him. Alert, intelligent eyes that peered sharply from under a deeply furrowed brow. A hooked beak-like nose and tight unrevealing lips. He was never still. And his hands gestured with quick darting little gestures, and as he ate curry he pecked daintily at his food. Oh, he was definitely a birdman, but what went on behind that impenetrable façade? Whom did he suspect? Was he even now gaining information at our expense?

Elly was pouring forth details of Mary's favourite dishes. 'Aah, she always loved my curry. Mary couldn't resist curry — many's the time I've taken her down a dish of it. And mushrooms. Oh, she'd eat those at any time. Why, she bought some on the day she was murdered, I remember Rosemary telling me. Didn't you, dear?'

I nodded. That remark painted a picture so vividly that I shut my eyes not to see Mary's slanting smile, as she stood in the market with me. The Inspector shot a penetrating look in my direction and said abruptly, 'This has been a very enjoyable encounter but I'm afraid I must say goodnight. I have work to do. If you will excuse me.'

'Of course,' Elly returned brightly, 'we must be going soon ourselves, don't let us keep you.'

He rose, and placing his chair correctly back in place, signalled to the waitress. 'Goodnight. Miss Moreland, Miss Lennox. I trust we shall meet again sometime, and continue our interesting conversation.' He bowed slightly and left.

'What an odious man!' Elly exclaimed, as soon as his back was turned.

I looked at her in some astonishment. 'Well, that's very cool, my pet, consider-ing you asked him to join us, and have been nattering away for the last half hour!'

'Oh, I thought he might tell us something, but he's such a dry old stick you can't get anything out of him.'

I sighed for Elly's simplicity and said: 'I think we had better make a move, dear. Can you see the waitress?' Elly waved at her, and after paying, we threaded our way through the tables to the door.

It seemed a shame to just catch the bus and go home, so heedless of expense, I hailed a passing taxi, which was fortunately empty, and bundled a shocked, protesting Elly into its capacious depths.

'The extravagance. The unnecessary extravagance!' was all I could get from her during the whole trip, but she had assumed the air of a visiting Duchess, when we got out at the flats, so I gathered that the taxi agreed with her.

The living room window of the Francis's flat faced the road, and I saw with a slight shock that the light was on. Elly saw it at the same time, and nudged my arm. 'Good gracious, John must be there. Fancy him staying up so late, it will only upset him. Perhaps, we should knock and make him come upstairs for a bit. It's not good to be down there alone.'

I demurred slightly, feeling reluctant to come between John and his memories. But Elly was not to be shaken. She knocked firmly on the door. We waited a minute but he didn't answer. I pulled her arm. 'Come away. He may not want us.'

She made no reply, but stood silent, a strange expression crossing her face. The next instant she began hammering on the door and calling his name, her voice loud and frightened. Appalled I tried to stop her, but she turned on me, her face working. 'Can't you smell it? Gas! It's coming from under the door! Run upstairs and see if Bob's there. We'll have to break the lock!'

I flew upstairs, my heart banging frantically, and nearly cannoned into Bob as he came racing down. 'What on earth's the row about?' he shouted.

'It's John! We can't make him hear, and there's a smell of gas!'

Not waiting for me to finish, he tore back up the stairs and returned, grasping the axe from the fire apparatus on the top landing. Elly was still knocking, and she stood back as Bob smashed violently at the panels. The wood splintered and broke, and thrusting his hand inside he twisted the handle and thrust the door open.

The smell of gas was very strong, and Bob's first action was to throw open the window. John was nowhere to be seen.

'He's in the bedroom!' Elly shouted, frantically, struggling with the door. It swung inwards abruptly. An overwhelming, sickening wave of gas enveloped us, and we saw John, lying back in a chair, his face turned towards the hissing unlit gas fire.

Somehow, heaven knows how, we turned it off, dragged his heavy body out into the passage, and propped him up, and fixed the swing doors back to let the life giving fresh air reach him. He was breathing, very, very faintly, but he was still breathing. Her hands shaking Elly rang 999 and asked for an ambulance. They were very quick, but it seemed like hours to me, before we heard the welcome clang of the alarm and the ambulance arrived.

No time was wasted. After a cursory glance at him, they fetched a stretcher and hurried him inside. A man took down all we could tell him, and said we would be notified later. Somebody called impatiently from the door, and with a hasty goodbye he was gone. The ambulance screamed away and left us standing white and bewildered until the final note faded into the distance.

Bob said quietly, 'I think we should let the Inspector know. You two go upstairs and I'll come up when I've got on to the station.'

We went into Elly's living room. Bob joined us with the news that the police were on their way, and we sat waiting. The minutes ticked by, slowly, wearily, until a sharp rap on the door made us start nervously. I opened the door.

It was the Inspector and two policemen. The preliminaries over, he stood looking down at us for a moment, then said thoughtfully, 'An unexpected meeting indeed.'

Unable to bear the suspense, I gulped out: 'John will be alright won't he, Inspector? We reached him in time, didn't we?'

'The hospital have this number and instructions to phone me should any change occur in his condition.'

'Oh dear,' I worried. 'I should never have let him come back here alone.'

'You knew he was coming, Miss Lennox?' he asked quickly.

'Yes. I met him in the park today; he said he wanted to clear things up. He was so strange and unlike himself — ' I stopped as I remembered his lonely words, and said in a low voice: 'Perhaps he found his own salvation.'

Bob murmured. 'I think I see what you mean.'

'You infer, I presume Mr. McDonnell, that he attempted to take his own life,' the Inspector said severely.

Bob shrugged. 'Well, it looks like it Inspector. He was terribly upset about Mary's death. It must have played on his mind, until he couldn't face it any longer.'

Elly was crying openly. 'His heart was

broken, we all knew it. I pray that the wicked person responsible for this is punished. Nothing's too bad for him.'

The Inspector moved restlessly. He was about to speak when the shrill clamour of the telephone ringing in the hall arrested him. A moment later a policeman reported that it was the hospital. He hurried out and we sat, frozen on our seats, eyes fixed on the door. There was a murmur of voices, the sound of the phone being replaced, then footsteps on the stairs. The door opened slowly and he came in.

'Well?' Bob burst out anxiously.

Inspector Nevil's glance included us all. 'I regret to tell you that Mr. Francis died without regaining consciousness, a few minutes ago.'

There was an awful pause, broken by the sound of Elly's sobs. A great weight seemed to have descended on my shoulders, as I moved slowly to comfort her.

A lot of activity was going on downstairs. We could hear men moving about in that room below and one came in to tell the inspector that there was no trace of a suicide note. 'Well keep looking,' he returned. 'There's bound to be a confession in some form or other.'

'A confession?' I gasped, mystified.

He turned and answered me, his tones level and deliberate. 'A confession, Miss Lennox. I do not assert this as a fact, but we cannot overlook the possibility that the reason for which John Francis took his life, was remorse.'

He bowed slightly. 'It has not apparently occurred to anyone in this room, that John Francis' suicide is tantamount to a confession of murdering his wife.'

4

Post mortem

Stephen phoned me about ten the next day. He had read the news of John's death in the morning papers. Their tone was guarded, but the implication of 'suicide after the murder of wife' was inevitable. 'Another terrible shock for you, my dear,' he said sympathetically. 'I wish you'd get out of that wretched place for a few days. Mother would be delighted for you to come and stay with us. Why don't you? I can pick you up this evening, on my way home from the office.'

It was sweet of him to worry. Yet somehow I did not really want to leave the others. We were all so closely bound up in the events of the past week, that it seemed like desertion to go away now. Besides, I very much doubted my ability to sustain such a visit — my nerves were too shaken. I excused myself as best I could.

'Well think it over,' he replied, 'the offer's still open. Anyway you'll be coming down at the weekend. I'll call in tonight to talk about it. Goodbye, Rosemary, take care of yourself.'

I hung up thoughtfully. The idea seemed tempting on a little reflection, and I almost phoned back to say I had changed my mind. Then a vision of that 'grand old lady', described so fondly by Stephen, and so caustically by Elly, arose in my mind's eye, and I decided to stay as I was!

The door of John and Mary's flat had been padlocked, and sealed by the police. They had been there nearly all night. When I went to bed, somewhere in the early hours of the morning, they were still down there searching for the confession note. Mercifully now they were gone, without the evidence they wanted. It was no surprise to me. I was very dubious as to the existence of such a note, and the implication thereof. Wearily I climbed the stairs, and I went back into my bedroom. No one was about, and I was very tired. I looked longingly at my warm bed, and after a little tussle with my conscience, took off my dressing gown and climbed back in.

I was asleep in a few minutes. It was not the deep sleep beloved of the poets, that brings comfort and peace. No. I tossed and struggled in the depths of a hideous nightmare. Mary's dead body rose from the floor, advancing towards me with piteously extended hands. John stood silently watching, his eyes blank, a rope round his neck, and through it all, came the menacing hiss of escaping gas. I must have screamed, for the next thing I knew was Elly bending over me saying soothingly, 'Wake up dear. Wake up, you're only dreaming.'

I clutched her hands in wild terror, and relaxed thankfully. She smiled kindly. 'You left your door open, so I just came in to see if everything was alright. My goodness, what a state you're in. I've made you some breakfast. Would you like me to bring it in, or do you want to get up?'

Elly's kindly presence was the best comfort I could have asked, and the thought of breakfast put new life into me, I hugged her gratefully, 'I'll get up, Elly, and thank you.'

The table was laid ready in the kitchen, and a cosy warmth mixed with the smell of bacon and coffee greeted me as I came out. I glanced at the clock.

'It's half past one,' she informed me, reading my mind, 'you've had enough sleep now, surely?' I hung my head in mock shame, and giggled. Elly in her schoolmarm mood, always made me want to laugh. She directed a severe look in my direction and then smiled. 'I've had no lunch, so I'll have something with you, if you behave sensibly, and don't carry on like that. She turned from the oven, two plates of egg and bacon in her hands, and put them quickly on the table. 'Mind they're hot! My eggs, your bacon. That makes us quits, eh?'

I poured her a cup of coffee. 'You're just back from Mrs. Samuels, I suppose Elly? My, you make me feel lazy, but I slept so badly last night.'

She nodded, and absently buttering a piece of toast, pushed it towards me. 'Yes,

I don't think any of us slept too well, but to tell you the truth, I was glad to be up and about. You're young, of course, you need your sleep. When you get to my age it's different.'

'Stephen phoned this morning. He wants me to stay at his home for a few days.'

'Ah now,' Elly beamed, 'that's just what you want, you've been through a lot, and the change will do you the world of good. I can see myself acting as caretaker to the entire block, at this rate. One of Bob's young ladies left a message asking if he'd like to go down to Kent this weekend. I mustn't forget to tell him when he comes.'

That, if I needed anything, decided me. 'You'll have company then. I'm not going.'

'Oh Rosemary! Stephen will be upset if you don't.'

'It's not him. It's his mother. I've heard some terrible things about her, and I'm sure she won't like me.'

'What a lot of nonsense!' Elly cried indignantly. 'The least you can do is go. Then decide for yourself, don't condemn the poor woman without a hearing.'

I shrugged irritably, though I had a sneaking feeling that Elly was quite right. To change the subject, I said sarcastically: 'I wonder which one of Bob's girl friends phoned him? As long as it wasn't that common blonde he should be pretty safe!'

'Bob safe? It's the other way around if you ask me. He's a terrible lady killer!'

'Bob!' I shook with mirth at the thought of Bob as a heartbreaker. He wasn't bad looking if you liked that type, but his manners and sense of humour, left a lot to be desired.

'Yes. You can laugh, Rosemary, but if I was thirty years younger and lived in the same block of flats, I wouldn't treat him as you do. You'll realize his worth one day and then it will be too late.'

I made a face at her, but she refused to be laughed out of it, and just sat there, shaking her head significantly at me. Seeing that she was really put out, I set myself to be pleasant and make her happy again. Dear Elly. It didn't take much effort, and she was soon bright and cheerful.

We washed up together, and then Elly left to do some shopping, the items listed neatly on a little pad in her bag. I did the housework, and then baked a sponge in Stephen's honour. By then the time was getting on and I changed into my second best dress. Jade green wool, with a plunging neckline. I preened in front of the mirror, putting the finishing touches and then gave a little start of excitement as Stephen knocked on the door. I opened it, stood on tiptoe, my eyes closed and murmured adoringly, 'Darling!'

I felt his powerful arms close tightly round me, then his mouth hard and firm against mine, as he kissed me. A long lingering kiss that made my heart race with excitement and my very toes tingle. I heaved an ecstatic sigh and reluctantly opened my eyes to gaze up at him. Dreamily I gazed — at an unruly black wave, a jutting chin and a pair of mocking brown eyes!

For a second I stared unbelievingly, then aiming a furious blow I leaped back and yelled. 'Bob McDonnell! How dare you! How dare you!'

Yes it was Bob! He gave a snort, a sort of smothered grunt, then threw back his head and laughed! Yes laughed, until the tears stood in his eyes and he was clutching weakly at the door handle for support! I went nearly off my head with rage! I had never been so angry in my life. I hit and punched at Bob's brawny figure, making as much impression as a fly, and yelled insults at the top of my voice.

He sobered up fast, and grabbing my wrists marched me inside and sat me down plump on the nearest chair. 'Now listen, poppet. Don't go up in the air like that! I didn't want to disappoint you. You looked so expectant! What was I to do?'

He started to laugh again, and with a terrific effort I got my temper under control, and said with a jerky smile. 'Alright, forget it,' adding a little unnecessarily, 'I thought it was Stephen.'

'So it is!' a voice called from the open door, and to add to my confusion in walked Stephen. 'Hello, Bob. Haven't seen you for ages. No don't go, I want your support.'

I directed a vindictive glare at Bob who

promptly ignored it, and settled himself in the best armchair. Stephen came over and kissed my hot cheek. 'Hello, darling. You look very nice. Glad to see you've got some colour back. How about a cup of tea for two tired business men?'

'Of course,' I replied, trying not to sound as flustered as I felt, 'it's all ready for you, darling. I don't suppose Bob wants any though. He has a date tonight. Haven't you Bob?'

Bob stretched his long legs, reached for his cigarette case, and said succinctly: 'No.' Shaking with fury I swept into the kitchen and left them to it.

When I came back, carrying the tray, Stephen was emphasizing something with forceful gestures, while Bob lay back behind a perfect smoke screen, nodding his head in sage agreement, from time to time. I put the tray down and began to pour out the tea. 'Would you like a piece of sponge, Stephen?' I asked.

He said he'd love a piece, and I watched with eager anticipation as he took his first bite. Bob, of course, had to interfere. 'If that's Elly's, I'll have a slice.'

'It isn't,' I said coldly. 'I made it myself.'

He grinned. 'Well, I'm not hungry anyway!' If looks could kill, Bob would have been prostrate, as I glared hatred at him; as they can't, of course, he remained comfortably seated by the fire.

Stephen saved the situation by saying it was delicious.

After a pause, he reached for my hand. 'Now Rosemary. I've been talking to Bob, and he agrees with me, that it would be best for you to get away for a few days. Staying, here won't serve any useful purpose. What do you say? Will you come?'

I sighed unhappily, wishing that Bob was anywhere but there, sitting opposite, and watching us with a fatherly expression. If only I could have Stephen to myself, to tell him a little of my shyness at the thought of meeting his mother. By some miracle Bob seemed to understand. He got up and smiling wisely, said he'd better be going. Elly had told him about the message from Freda — I sniffed superciliously, Freda was the blonde

— and he wanted to phone her. I quelled my curiosity to know if he was going to accept, said goodnight, and mercifully he went.

Left alone with Stephen, I began my explanations. He heard me out patiently and as I came to a faltering stop, chuckled and pulled me on his lap.

'Well, if that's all that's worrying you, my dear, you can stop right now, and start packing. No one would be shy with mother. She puts you at your ease in a moment. She's the sweetest person, Rosemary, and I know you'll love each other. Then Shelia will be popping in and out — '

'Shelia?'

'Yes. We grew up together. You'll adore her. She's a grand sport.' I felt convinced that I should do nothing of the kind. 'Grand sports' were definitely not my type. I was getting quite desperate, as the well-meant trap closed in tighter, and just as I was searching for a really final sort of excuse, there was a bang on the door.

It was Bob again. This was too much. My politeness strained to the limit, I said in my iciest tones: 'Well? What is it this time?'

He glanced apologetically at Stephen. 'I'm very sorry to interrupt you both, but this is serious. Inspector Nevil just phoned up, he says there's been a new development in the case, and will we please hold ourselves ready for questioning. He's on his way now. I said I'd warn you and Elly, Rosemary. I'm afraid you won't be able to go with Stephen just yet. I don't like the sound of things at all.'

This was a bombshell! 'Whatever can he want with us now?' I asked, mystified.

Bob shrugged. 'Search me, but he was very serious about it.'

'It's most inconsiderate of the man,' Stephen grunted. 'Does he expect you to hang around here for ever, at his command? I thought the whole affair was over and done with.' He rose and began putting on his coat. 'Well, I'd better go. He won't want me. I'm sorry Rosemary. Perhaps we'd better leave it till the weekend after all.'

I went downstairs with him and watched until the car had turned the corner. When I got back, Elly had come in from next door, and we all sat around, finishing up the tea and sponge, amidst the wildest conjecture, Elly convinced that the police had found the real murderer, and that justice was finally to be done. The sound of a car drawing up outside put an effective end to the conversation, and I ran to the door to admit the Inspector and his attendant constable. We gazed at him expectantly and he began speaking in a severe, abrupt voice.

'A post mortem was performed today on the body of the late John Francis. We considered it a mere formality, but the resulting evidence has completely disproved this theory.' He drew a sheet of notepaper from his wallet. 'John Francis died as we know from gas poisoning — what we didn't know was that a large quantity of laudanum was found present in the body.' There was a pause, and his sharp eyes flashed. 'This quantity had been recently administered, from which we infer, that he was heavily drugged before he breathed in any of the gas.'

I gazed at him blankly not understanding. Elly muttered something unintelligible, but Bob jumped to his feet and cried incredulously: 'You can't mean — '

'Thank heaven someone takes my meaning,' the Inspector said dryly. 'An unconscious man cannot get off his chair, and turn on his own gas fire. No. John Francis was deliberately and cleverly murdered!'

5

At the Blue Cellar

A complete babel broke out at his statement. John murdered? We were all talking together, almost shouting, when Inspector Nevil silenced us with an authoritative wave of his hand.

'You all understand the situation now, and I must ask you to give me the full details again. We start from another angle this time. Miss Lennox, you were the last one to see him I believe. Tell me in your own words what happened.'

I told him all I could remember about our meeting in the park, and he checked it again carefully against my previous statement. 'Yes, yes. You did not return to your flat until the evening. Then you were accompanied by Miss Moreland?'

'That's quite right.'

'Thank you. Now Miss Moreland — '

'You saw nothing of him during the

afternoon,' I put in eagerly.

'At what time did you come back?' he asked, ignoring my interruption.

'Let me see now, Inspector. I had a cup of tea in the café, and met Mrs. Edwards from across the road about five I suppose.'

'Was Mr. Francis in his flat then?'

'I don't think so. There was no light on and I couldn't hear anybody in there. No, I don't see how he could have been.'

'Thank you.' He turned to Bob 'You were here all evening, Mr. McDonnell?'

'Yes.'

'Was there a light showing when you came in?'

'Yes there was. That would be around seven o'clock. I didn't like to interfere, or push myself, so I just went upstairs to my flat.'

'You heard nothing, during the course of the evening.'

'No, I wouldn't unless it was pretty loud. Mine is the top flat, and you don't get much noise. I was writing the whole time; I remember thinking how uncannily silent it was.'

Inspector Nevil and the constable spoke together for a few minutes, comparing notes. Apparently everything was satisfactory so far. Armed with a fresh file, he began again. 'Miss Moreland first noticed the smell of gas, and hammered on the door. That would be at eleven, when Miss Lennox and Miss Moreland returned together.' He smiled slightly. 'You are both fortunate in that I can supply you with a partial alibi.'

'Good Heavens! You don't think any of us did it?' Elly cried in astonishment.

'I don't think anything at all,' he returned with some asperity. 'I am merely trying to establish facts. You must look at it this way, Madam. Mary Francis is murdered. Everyone can give a reasonable account of themselves, except her husband. He admits that they had quarrelled, and that he was the last one to see his wife alive. Then a few days later, he himself is discovered dying in a gas-filled room. The implication is obvious. I in fact considered the case closed. But now in the light of this new evidence, we must start all over again. Two murders have been committed, and we seek a clever, devilish killer. One without scruples or mercy, who may, for all we know, strike again.'

Elly shivered and said in a faint voice: 'You make it sound so frightening.'

He relaxed a little. 'I'm sorry, that is not my intention. I just want you to realize and understand, why we must ask all these questions. We must check and recheck everything that has been done and said. One of you three may hold the key — unwittingly, but you may hold it. Each of you was present at the finding of both bodies, and are the only people who can help us.'

Bob had been sitting quietly listening; now he looked up and said: 'How about the Club 'The Blue Cellar' where they worked? Have you made any inquiries there?'

The Inspector looked pained. 'Naturally, we have not overlooked that side of their lives. I was, as a matter of fact, somewhat struck by the attitude of the bandleader, a Mr. Les Roberts. He was very upset over Mary Francis' death, more so than one would expect from a business acquaintance.'

I racked my brains trying to recall something Mary had said on that last day. Then it came to me. 'That was the man they quarrelled over!' I cried eagerly.

'Indeed! Mr. Francis was jealous?'

'Yes, but Mary said he was silly and that there was nothing in it.'

Inspector Nevil noted this down and the questions required and putting away his pen handed the file to the constable. 'Now, my friends. If you will be good enough to come downstairs, we can go over your evidence on the spot.' We got up a little stiffly and followed him.

There was another policeman now waiting outside the Francis' flat. He opened the door, and stood aside for us to enter, then closed it, and we heard him slip the padlock back into position. The police had been busy while the Inspector was questioning us. Doors and cupboards were open, and seated, busily sorting through a pile of correspondence by the bureau was a policeman.

'Anything new, Thompson?'

'No, sir,' the policeman answered smartly. 'Seems to be the usual stuff, letters and bills. Nothing much to go on, I'm afraid.'

'Hmm. Oh well, keep trying.'

He led us into the bedroom. Everything looked so different. The gas fire had been ticketed, and placed in the corner. A glass with lipstick stains on the rim stood beside it, and all the furniture had been moved round. Elly peered at the glass in a fascinated way. 'Is that what he took the laudanum in?' she asked breathlessly.

'I don't know. We are taking it with us for examination. It was left on the draining board in the kitchen.'

Elly retired, looking deeply impressed.

We all went through our stories again. Very macabre it seemed to stand in that ordinary room, describing the terrible things it had seen. I was thankful when the ordeal was over and Inspector Nevil intimated that we could go back. He accompanied us, and paused for a few final words. 'I want you to take care. If you recall or notice anything, connected with the case, however trivial, get in touch with me. Don't take any chances. Above all, don't discuss the case with outsiders.'

Bob said levelly, 'You don't think there's any danger, Sir?'

'No, I don't say that. I merely ask for a little caution. We are dealing with a killer, and cannot be too careful.'

Listening to him, I resolved to speak. Screwing up my courage I blurted out. 'Inspector Nevil — '

'Yes, Miss Lennox?'

'You did say trivial?'

'My dear young lady, speak up. This is no time for hesitation, if you know anything.'

I made up my mind. 'Well, I don't exactly know anything, but Sunday night just as I was getting ready for bed, somebody tried my door. I've been trying to think it was imagination, but in the face of all this — ' I stopped and watched his face anxiously. He was very serious.

'Did you open the door?'

'Yes. I called out first, and then as there was no reply, I unlocked it. There wasn't a sign of anybody. The corridor was deserted.'

'At what time?'

'About half past eleven. I had been with Bob all day, and I remember the time particularly, as I left him at eleven, and it always takes me half an hour to get to bed.'

The grave face relaxed, and he smiled slightly. 'Don't let it worry you, but if it occurs again, don't open the door, and phone me as soon as you can.'

'I wish you'd wakened me, Rosemary,' Elly said worriedly, 'being frightened like that all by yourself. You could have knocked on the wall. I'd have heard you.'

'I will next time,' I said fervently.

'Well, let us hope that there is no next time,' Inspector Nevil said quite kindly. 'Now I must bid you all goodnight. You will be seeing me again.' With which cryptic remark he made his departure.

The door had barely closed behind him, when Elly fled to my kitchen to make some life saving tea, and Bob swore at me. 'Why the devil didn't you tell me about this at the time?' he said angrily, fumbling for a cigarette. 'Anything might have happened.'

'That's just why I didn't tell you. Nothing happened, and I know how you and Elly would make a fuss.'

'Fuss!' Bob exploded, and charging into the kitchen after Elly, demanded what she thought. Elly had a great deal to say on the subject, including the fact that we might all have been murdered in our beds, through my lack of sense.

'You open that door to anyone, Rosie,' Bob said, and grinned suddenly. I felt my colour rise. 'Like tonight now — '

'Kettle's boiling!' I interrupted hastily, my cheeks scarlet, and clattered round with the teapot and caddy. He gave me a wicked look, but no more.

We carried the tea into the living room, and settled down to discussing everything Inspector Nevil had said or done.

'It must have been someone they both knew and trusted, because there was no sign of breaking anywhere,' Elly murmured. We agreed on this and racked our brains for clues. None came. I fell to wondering about the policemen downstairs.

'Have they all gone?' I asked Bob.

He opened the door and peered over the banisters. 'There's one left. I can see him through the glass doors; he's standing just outside the entrance.' This was a very comforting thought. No one could get in or out, without being seen and questioned, I felt reassured.

After a while Elly finished her tea. 'I think I'll be getting off to bed. I'm too tired and bewildered to stay up any longer. But don't forget dear, knock on the door if you want me. I'll hear.'

I kissed her goodnight, promised to wake her if necessary, and satisfied, she left, patting Bob on the shoulder. He stayed a few minutes longer and then went too.

I puttered about in the flat clearing up, my mind busy. Oddly enough I didn't think about the police or the murder. I suppose the human mind can take just so many shocks; after that it refuses to function properly and reverts to normal things as a sort of safety valve. No, I thought of Stephen, and how he had said I looked nice, of his concern for me. I wondered what the girls at the office would say when they read the papers tomorrow morning, then going back to Stephen again, whether he had believed that I had made the sponge and if he really thought it was delicious.

By the time I climbed into bed, I was very tired. I put the light out and lay smiling to myself in the dark. A blissful sense of peace hovered round me — I think the policeman on the door had a lot to do with it — and turning over with a sleepy sigh, was asleep almost at once.

I dreamed of Stephen. In my dream he was waving to me from the corner. I ran towards him laughing, but when I reached him and put out my arms, I found it was Bob McDonnell I was embracing.

⋆   ⋆   ⋆

It was raining heavily the next day. Streaming down the windows and lashing spitefully against the wall in a dismal rhythm. I switched the radio on to drown the noise and prepared my breakfast feeling rather solitary. Elly would be out all day. Every Wednesday she went to visit a cousin in Pinner — her relations were scattered everywhere it seemed, some of them in the most unlikely places — and she would not be home until late evening. I was going to miss her. In some ways I wished I was back at the office. In fact, I had almost decided to phone Stephen and tell him I would be in later, when Bob knocked.

'Are you up yet, Rosie?' he called.

I hastened him in. 'It's half past nine. You'll be terribly late for work,' I informed him.

'I'm not going.'

'Not going?'

'No, I just phoned and asked if they would let me have the morning off. I worked over the bank holiday, so they were quite gracious about it.'

'Oh well, sit down and have some — '

'Tea and toast?' He laughed. 'The diet round here is rather monotonous but as you insist . . . '

I tried to curb my curiosity as to what he was planning to do with his free time, but it was too much for me. Pouring him out a cup of tea and rising to fetch another cup for myself, I asked casually: 'Going somewhere special?'

Bob shook his head and sat silently gazing at the table then apparently making up his mind he answered: 'We're all in a devil of a situation. As far as I can see the police haven't got a thing to go on. They thought John killed Mary, and now that he's been killed too, they're stuck with the case. Something's got to be done, and quickly.'

'Well, you can't do anything,' I interposed rudely.

'Perhaps not, but I'm going to have a try!'

'What do you mean — a try?'

'I got on to Inspector Nevil this morning and told him some cock-a-hoop story about leaving a book I needed in John's room. He said it would be O.K. for me to fetch it. The constable gave me the padlock key — apparently he's going. They've finished in there now, so I can go ahead.'

'But what's the point of it all?'

'I'm going to search the place myself.

I've tried to remember everything John said the night he slept in my flat. That could be a help, anyway. I might stumble on something they've overlooked.'

He lit a cigarette and gazed rather defiantly at me. The more I thought about his plan, the more it appealed to me. Detective stories have always been my weakness, and here we were, living out a real life thriller. I grabbed my chance and said eagerly. 'Oh Bob, let me come with you. I'm sure I could help. After all, I was the last one to talk to them both.'

He shook his head decisively. 'No, you keep out of this. I wish I hadn't mentioned it now, I might have known you'd start interfering and getting wild ideas.'

'I'm not keeping out, and it's no use you trying to make me. I'm coming, and if you say 'No' again, I'll phone the inspector and tell him what you're up to!'

We argued back and forth for the next half hour, but my continual browbeating, and threats finally wore him down, and very reluctantly he agreed to let me help. The point was, I hung over the banisters, reported that the policeman was not in sight, and proposed we commence operations at once.

We went quietly downstairs. My heart was pounding with excitement as I watched Bob insert the key, and the padlock clicked open. He put them both in his pocket, and we slipped into the room, shutting the door and wedging it with a chair. Thus secured, against surprise, we looked at each other rather helplessly, at a loss where to begin. Bob settled the matter. 'You take the kitchen Rosie, and I'll look around here to start with.'

The kitchen had a very innocent appearance, there seemed nothing capable of being construed as the smallest clue. The larder was as good a place to begin as anywhere, so I opened it cautiously, and peered inside. It was well stocked, with tins and packet foods, but there was obviously nothing of any value to our search. I closed it, and turned my attention to the rest of the furniture. A cream painted rubbish bin caught my eye. It stood under the sink, and pulling it out, I poked at the contents. A few empty tins, some stale bread, and vegetable peelings wrapped in paper. Again a blank. I was just going to push it back, when I noticed two buttons lying at the side of one of the tins. Excitedly I picked them out and called for Bob. 'Look,' I said proudly. 'A man's coat buttons. Do you think they belong to the murderer? Perhaps Mary pulled them off in the struggle.'

He was sceptical. 'I can't see any self respecting murderer carefully putting his buttons in the rubbish bin, my pet. They're probably John's thrown away for some reason.'

He went back into the living room and I slipped the buttons absently into my pocket and continued to search. No clues appeared and I was just gazing disconsolately into the larder again, when a shout from Bob sent me tearing eagerly into the other room.

'What is it? What is it? Have you got something?'

'I think I have!' He held up a half smoked cigar stub. 'Look at the band.'

I took it from him gingerly, and

examined the band. It was gold embossed with the letters 'B.C.' in blue.

''Blue Cellar'! The name of the club where they worked, and John never smoked a cigar in his life, he hated the things!'

I gazed back at him joyfully. 'Where did you find it?'

'Under the waste paper basket. They must have missed it last night.'

Greatly elated, we decided to retire with our prize and talk over the next move upstairs. Back in my flat, Bob put the evidence in an envelope, and carefully sealed and pocketed it. Then we got down to business. There was no doubt in either of our minds as to the ownership of that cigar butt. It was Les Roberts. The man John and Mary had quarrelled over. Bob stated the facts one by one, and I couldn't help thinking, how like Inspector Nevil he sounded.

'Let's just suppose that Mary was involved with this man. Perhaps the quarrel she mentioned was really because John had found out. We can imagine his state of mind, and that evening, if our supposition is correct, he would certainly have tackled Les Roberts about it. These bandleaders get plenty of rests between numbers. They never play right through the evening, non-stop. Roberts could have slipped away, to see Mary and discuss things. Women are funny. Perhaps she'd changed her mind and didn't want anything more to do with him. They quarrelled and he lost control and killed her. Right. He'd hurry back, probably no one had even missed him, and carry on as if nothing had happened. When the police questioned him he got frightened, and in an effort to put the blame on John he drugged and gassed him. He wouldn't think of an autopsy giving him away.'

He paused for breath, leaving me quite awestruck at his reasoning. It all fitted, every little item dovetailed neatly into place. The Inspector's words drifted across my mind: 'Anything, however trivial — get in touch with me'. Hesitantly, I murmured. 'Shouldn't we tell the police, Bob?'

He shook his head. 'Not yet. We've got to have more to go on. We can't go charging into the Police Station, and accuse someone on the strength of a half smoked cigar. No, I think I'll take a look at this Mr. Roberts tonight.'

'You mean you're going to the 'Blue Cellar'? I'm coming too, Bob! I'm not being left out of it now!'

'I don't suppose it's of any use trying to stop you, and it will seem more natural if we go together. They'll think we're just another couple out for the evening.'

He glanced at the clock. 'I'd better be on my way to the office. See you tonight, then. I'll pick you up at eight o'clock.' He wheeled round abruptly in the doorway. 'And Rosie, don't discuss this with outsiders. We can't be too careful.'

In the afternoon the rain cleared up. I had to do something to take my mind off the coming evening so I went shopping. Too excited to bother about cooking food, I had a combined lunch and tea at the corner café and hung around willing the time to pass Finally, my patience gave out and I hurried home.

Needless to say, I was ready long before eight. I read a novel, smoked endless cigarettes, and could settle to nothing. Bob must have been equally worked up, because he arrived a quarter of an hour early and made no comment on the fact that I too, was ahead of schedule.

We hailed a taxi and directed it to the Blue Cellar. I grasped Bob's arm in a convulsive attempt to steady myself, and even his voice was a little strained as he said: 'For heaven's sake control yourself Rosie, or you'll give the game away in the first five minutes.'

'No, I won't. I'm as cool as a cucumber really.' He gave me a sceptical glance, and I rushed on: 'Have you ever been there before?'

'No but I can imagine what it will be like.'

'What?'

'Shockingly expensive!' He grinned comically and before I could reply, the taxi pulled up with a grinding of brakes.

'Here we are Sir. The Blue Cellar,' the driver announced. I don't know what his thoughts were, but he leered at me in a particularly suggestive way. I returned the leer with an expression of haughty disdain, and climbed out in my most dignified manner.

I left Bob and put my coat in the cloakroom. Normally, I would have spent time on my appearance, but tonight I gave my nose a brief powdering and left it at that. He was waiting by the door and a few minutes later, we were seated in a little 'trough' affair at the side of the floor facing the band. I glanced around me curiously. It was a very small place. Oblong in shape, with about twenty tables jutting out from the walls, each hidden from the other by a low partition. The lighting was provided by imitation candles set in amber coloured bottles on the tables, and discreetly shaded sidelights. The walls were pale blue merging into a deep midnight ceiling, dotted with silver stars. It was uncommonly like a cellar but the effect was rather bizarre.

Although we were early, there was quite a few couples dancing, and the air was already thick with smoke. A waiter glided up for our order and Bob said. 'Let's dance to this one, then we can get a good look at the band.'

It was a slow foxtrot and I was pleasantly surprised to find Bob an excellent partner. We drifted gently to the music for a bit and then began to move in the direction of a raised platform at the end of the room, where Les Roberts and his band beat out the rhythm.

He was a tall man, with black hair, thickly oiled and a small moustache. He laughed and joked with his 'boys' and occasionally called out a greeting to someone he recognized on the dance floor. A very attractive man, with an easy smooth charm. I began to understand John's jealousy. Quiet and retiring, he would have been no match for match for such vitality.

The music stopped with a prolonged roll on the drums and we went back to our table. 'Well? What do you think of him?' I queried, accepting a cigarette.

Bob shrugged. 'Bit of a dago. Not much good I should say.'

'Are you going to talk to him?'

He shrugged again. 'I don't know. I don't see how I can yet. Perhaps there'll be a chance later on. Oh, good. Here comes our soup.'

The evening wore on. The air got thicker and thicker, and the music louder, and more insistent. We danced a lot, and after a few drinks, the tension went and I relaxed and quite enjoyed myself.

We were sitting smoking and talking in low tones, when a waiter suddenly appeared at Bob's elbow and murmured something. I saw Bob's eyes flicker and he said: 'Certainly. Tell him to come over and have a drink with us.'

'Who?' I hissed. 'Who's coming over?'

He was excited. 'Les Roberts just asked if we'd mind if he joined us for a few minutes!'

6

Doubts and suspicions

Raising my eyes, I saw the figure of the bandleader coming towards us. I gripped my hands together tightly beneath the table and waited.

Bob stood up as he approached, and motioned him to a seat. 'This is an unexpected pleasure Mr. Roberts. Will you have a drink?' He signalled to the waiter.

Les Roberts' face was very white. 'Forgive me if I'm intruding,' he said stiffly, 'but I recognized you as friends of Mrs. Francis. I've seen you both at the flats from time to time.'

This was news to me, but I said nothing. He went on speaking. 'I'm glad you came. I want to hear everything. Mr. and Mrs. Francis were old friends of mine. I can hardly realize that they're both dead — so cruelly dead. If there's anything I can do, any help I can give, please tell me.' Bob had listened quietly to this, but he made no comment. There was a strained pause and Roberts continued: 'What I mean is, you've both seen the police since John's death. You know how things are going, whom they suspect — ' His voice trailed off.

Bob answered very levelly. 'We know nothing Mr. Roberts. The police aren't exactly communicative, and I suppose in a way, everyone connected with the case is suspect.'

The waiter brought along the drinks then. Les Roberts drained his glass at a gulp and sat playing nervously with the glass. 'I believe they think I did it,' he burst out suddenly.

I felt a sudden pity for him. 'You mustn't think that. We all feel that the police are concentrating on us personally.'

He smiled faintly. 'But not everyone had my motive.' Bob and I stiffened slightly, and he smiled again, half mockingly. 'Oh yes, I had a motive. I was in love with Mary. Been in love with her for years.' He fumbled for a cigarette and I saw how his hands shook.

Blowing out a cloud of smoke, he went on sombrely: 'She knew it of course, so did John. I might have stood a chance, but for him. She liked me, I'm sure of that. The boys used to tease him about us. It was common knowledge — '

Bob shifted uncomfortably, but his voice was kind. 'That's no reason for killing them both. Besides, you've got a foolproof alibi. You were here all the time, in full view of about fifty people. I shouldn't worry.'

'I went back to my flat that night, to get one of the numbers. I was only twenty minutes but long enough. So there goes my alibi.'

'What did the police say to that?'

'I haven't told them yet. Don't know why I'm telling you. I must get over to the band. Here's my phone number. I'd appreciate it, if you'd let me know how things are going. I hope you have a pleasant evening. Goodnight.'

Bob whistled softly under his breath as we watched Les Roberts walk away. 'Well, what do you make of that, Rosie?'

I shook my head. 'I don't know. He

seemed to be telling the truth, didn't he?'

Bob agreed. 'Funny to trust complete strangers like that. If he wanted to keep it from the police you'd think he'd be more careful.'

We sat talking, and as the band struck up a waltz, Bob said: 'Come on pet, one more dance, and we'll get out of this place, eh?' They had lowered the lights and we drifted slowly round to the music. I thought of Stephen. How gaily he and I had danced, that Saturday night, never dreaming of the terrible events to come.

We passed the music dais, where a young girl was crooning softly down the mike and I thought of Mary. How lovely she must have looked up there, singing. And smiling her slanting smile.

The music stopped with the inevitable drum-roll, and I came out of my reverie as Bob piloted me back to the table. We were both weary of the Blue Cellar, and I retired to the cloakroom to collect my things. When I came back, I found Bob talking to a man around his own age.

'This is Michael Gerrard,' Bob introduced, as I came up and the man glanced at me. 'We once did the same College course — quite a few years ago, now.'

'Pleased to meet you,' I said guardedly.

'We haven't seen each other since College days,' Bob said.

'Thought I saw you here last week, old man,' Michael Gerrard observed. 'Only I wasn't quite sure then, so didn't introduce myself.'

'Me? Lord, no. I've never been here before tonight.'

'Must have made a mistake.' Thereafter conversation languished, and we exchanged farewells and left.

★   ★   ★

As we returned to the flats and climbed the stairs, Elly's door opened and she called out: 'Oh, there you are at last. That wretched Inspector Nevil has been here and I've had all the questions to myself!'

She had some coffee waiting, but Bob wouldn't stop long; he said he had some writing or something to do. So I thanked him for a pleasant evening and said goodnight.

The Inspector had reported nothing new. He had just dropped in to see if all was well. I giggled at Elly. 'I'll bet he came round for some of that home cooking you were telling him about.'

She chuckled. 'I wouldn't put it past him. He certainly did full justice to my curry.'

'There — what did I tell you?'

She looked pleased and stirred her coffee. 'I'm glad to see you're taking my advice, Rosemary.'

'What advice?'

'About Bob.'

'Bob? Oh, you old matchmaker! There's nothing like that about it. We were doing a bit of sleuthing!' I told her all about our search that morning, and the cigar with the blue band. 'So we decided to investigate and see Les Roberts for ourselves,' I finished.

Elly was very interested. 'What was he like?'

I thought for a moment. 'I can't quite make my mind up about him. He admitted being in love with Mary. He hinted that with John out of the way he'd have stood a chance. He even told us that he'd lied to the police about leaving the club that night she was murdered, yet somehow I liked him. I felt sorry for him in a way.'

Elly pursed her lips. 'Why should he tell you all that? He might know you'd have to tell the police if they questioned you about him.'

Again I was stumped. 'I think he needed to tell someone,' I said rather lamely.

'Hmph. He sounds a very suspicious character to me. You ought to be more careful. The Inspector was very insistent on that point, and he warned us all,' she said.

'I know. I said that to Bob, but he wouldn't let me phone this morning. He thought we'd look a couple of fools if we went down to the station with nothing more than a cigar butt as evidence.'

'Well, I shall speak to Bob. If he wants to get killed off I don't, and I'm sure to get drawn into it, one way or another.' She sighed and I smiled to myself. It was so true. Poor Elly got involved in everything without lifting a finger.

We began to clear up. 'Oh my goodness!' she exclaimed. 'I nearly forgot, child. Your young man phoned up this evening.'

'Stephen! You didn't tell him where I was?'

'How could I? I didn't know myself. I simply said you were out and would he call tomorrow or leave a message.'

I breathed again. 'Did he leave any message?'

She eyed me archly. 'Just his love. Isn't that enough?'

I hugged her, nearly dropping the sugar basin, and gulped: 'Quite enough, thank you, Elly darling.'

Elly teased me a lot after that, and when we had finished the washing up, said it was high time I was in bed. She stood in her open doorway and watched me safely inside.

'Knock on the wall if you want me, Rosemary. Goodnight, dear.'

I climbed into bed. Elly had given me a pile of American magazines a few weeks ago, and so far I hadn't had a chance to look at them. Propped up comfortably I started flicking through their glossy pages.

After reading about thirty advertisements, urging one to smoke various brands of tobacco, I was mesmerised into wanting a cigarette, and reached out a lazy hand for my case. The lighter as usual was not in working order, and I was forced to leave my warm bed and search in my other handbag until I found a box of matches.

Back in bed, armed with the ashtray for good measure, I went on reading, but something at the back of my mind was worrying me, and I couldn't concentrate. Eventually I gave up the attempt, and tried to think what it was. A picture was forming slowly in my brain. I could see the Blue Cellar, the band, the dancing couples, the tables — The tables? It came to me then in a flash. Every table had a box of matches fixed above the ashtray. A box covered in blue paper with 'B.C.' stamped on it in gold.

I picked up the box I had taken from my handbag. The one Bob had given me in Charlie's a few nights ago. It was

113

exactly the same!

Completely puzzled, I gazed at it. Bob said that he had never been to the Blue Cellar before tonight, yet he had given me these, last Sunday. That friend we had met, who thought he had seen Bob there last week — A little shiver went through me and Inspector Nevil's words came back with added emphasis, 'One of you three may hold the key to it all. Take no chances!'

The blue matchbox was still clutched in my hand when I woke next morning. In a sudden gust of anger I flung it across the room. It had given me a restless night and a troubled mind. This case must be getting me down, when I began to suspect Bob on the strength of a stupid little clue like that.

There were a thousand and one explanations for its being in his possession. Mary or John could have given it to him weeks ago. He might have found it, and absently pocketed it. Oh, I was just looking for trouble.

Viciously kicking the pile of magazines out of my way, I got up and made some tea. It was only half past seven, and I quailed at the prospect of another idle day. My 'rest cure' was in a fair way to killing me with boredom. I thought of Sally and the rest of the girls at the office with positive affection. There must be an awful lot of work to do at the office — Stephen would be there too — I decided to go back at once!

The decision made, my spirits lifted magically, and by the time I was ready to leave, I found myself really looking forward to a hard day's work! Obviously I was a born toiler.

The newspaper boy on the corner was yelling unintelligibly and waving his newspapers in the faces of the bus queue. I bought one. Taking my place, I glanced casually at the headlines. A political scandal had driven our case right off the front page, and there was only a slight mention of it inside. A column further down caught my eye. I gave a little gasp and gripped the paper tightly. 'Les Roberts, Band Leader, involved in car crash. Early this morning Mr. Roberts well-known band leader from the Blue

Cellar was seriously injured. He was taken to St. George's Hospital, where his condition is reported as very grave'.

Half an hour later I was outside the hospital. Of course, I was too early for visiting hours — I didn't even know if they'd let me see him, but I could at least make some inquiries.

The porter told me to wait, and obedient to his instructions I sat twisting my gloves. After a long time he returned, accompanied by a nurse. She spoke kindly: 'Are you a relation, Miss Lennox?'

'No, only a friend. I read about the accident, and came to see how he was.'

She frowned slightly. 'I'm afraid you won't be able to see him yet. The doctors are still with him. But if you'll care to come with me and wait in the visitors' room, I'll let you know if you can go in, when they've finished.'

She led me down a labyrinth of passages until we reached a door labelled 'Visitors'. I went in. It was a very severe room. Chairs lined the walls, and there was a large table, bare, except for a medical journal. Still it was warm and I sat down, prepared for a long wait.

Ten minutes passed and the door opened again, to admit a small dark-haired girl. She took the chair opposite me, and stared out of the window.

I glanced at her curiously. There was something familiar to me about her, but I couldn't place where I had seen her before. She looked round at that moment and caught my glance. Flushing awkwardly, I said: 'Excuse me staring but I thought I knew you.'

'No, we've never met, but I have seen you. You came to the Blue Cellar last night.'

I stared openly now. 'The Blue Cellar! Oh — I remember. Aren't you the vocalist with — '

'Les Roberts? Yes, I took over a few days ago.' She smiled faintly. 'It's a small world isn't it?'

I felt suddenly foolish. Obviously we were both here on the same errand. This girl at least, had some right but I had only met the man once, and here I was foisting myself into his private life. I should never have come.

Some instinct had drawn me on, the feeling that he would be lonely and friendless, and would welcome my visit.

As if divining my thoughts, she moved restlessly on the hard chair and said, 'I had to see him. The report said he was gravely ill. I was so worried.'

'I know. It was a terrible thing to read just like that. I only came to enquire, we're not old friends, or anything. I knew his other singers, that's why we were at the club last night.' I stumbled on with my explanations, getting more and more involved. Turning to her rather desperately in the midst of a long sentence, I saw to my horror that she was crying.

She made a little gesture, to hide her tears, and fumbled for a handkerchief. My heart melted towards this girl. She was young. About eighteen, I suppose. Her hair was untidy and she had obviously dressed in a hurry. Everything spoke of anxiety and haste and now while I burbled on, she had broken down into those piteous tears I went over and put my arm about her. She sobbed against my shoulder like a child and I held her tight until the storm passed.

Sitting up straight she wiped her eyes and gave me a watery little smile. 'Thank you. I'm better now. It's not knowing how he is.'

There was a rigid 'No smoking' notice on the wall, but I ignored it and offered her a cigarette, my own hands shaking as I held the match. 'He'll be alright,' I said reassuringly. 'You mustn't upset yourself so. He wouldn't want you to.'

'He wouldn't want anybody to be upset,' she sighed hopelessly. 'He probably doesn't want to live anyway,' her voice quickened. 'For years he's been in love with another woman. He never noticed me, of course I was only a kid, but I always loved him. This other woman she was the one you knew. The singer, who was killed. I thought he was getting over it. He took a bit of time teaching me, he said I was growing up. I began to hope — and then all that terrible tragedy happened, and he was heartbroken for her.' She shivered, then went on:

'I've been so wicked. Do you know how I felt?' her voice dropped to a whisper. 'In my heart I was glad! Glad that she was dead. I knew he'd need another vocalist quickly, and I was ready to take my chance. To take her place. And now — '

The tears came again.

I soothed her as best I could. Poor little thing, she was so desperate, so unhappy. If only we could get some news. This waiting was unendurable. As if in answer to my prayer, the door opened. The nurse who had spoken to me came in briskly. We gazed at her speechlessly, and to my great relief she smiled. 'Mr. Roberts is out of danger and can have a brief, very brief visit. Only a few minutes now, and only one of you, I'm afraid. Now, who is it to be?'

I picked up my handbag. 'This young lady has first claim. Thank you for bringing us the good news so quickly, nurse.' The tearful dark haired girl gave me a grateful glance.

I patted her arm. 'Go ahead. Everything's going to be alright now,' and watched as she followed the nurse across the hall. My own eyes were suspiciously moist, and I gave them a surreptitious pat with my handkerchief as I left the hospital.

It was eleven o'clock. To go in to the office now would create a stir, so perhaps it was best to make it tomorrow. I had just turned away when a man's voice hailed me, and to my astonishment I saw Inspector Nevil standing by the hospital steps. A thousand guilty thoughts rushed through my mind as I greeted him, and his opening remark did nothing to allay my fears. 'Good morning, Miss Lennox. I have been waiting for you, you see!'

'I'm just going to work!' I lied hastily.

He smiled 'So late? I don't think that would be very wise. Why not let me take you home? I should like to have a little talk with you.' Impossible to do anything but agree, and accompany him.

We arrived at my flat, and I left him in the living room, while I put some coffee on. Spruce and neat in a dark grey over-coat, as always, his personality invaded the room. Silently I handed him his cup and sat like a guilty criminal awaiting judgment while he drank it.

He gave me an oblique glance. 'I was not aware that you were in any way connected with Mr. Roberts?'

'I'm not really. I only met him last night. When I saw the accident in the papers. I thought I'd inquire how he was.'

'Indeed?' He cleared his throat and I saw that the time had surely come. 'Now, Miss Lennox, let us not beat about the bush. I want the whole story with nothing held back. A few days ago, you had never seen the man, yet today I find you at the hospital, obviously upset. How did it all come about?'

I hated to tell him, but the truth couldn't be held back any longer. Quietly I explained. How Bob and I had decided to investigate, how we had found the cigar butt and gone to the Blue Cellar, and talked with Les Roberts. He heard me out, never interrupting, but letting me tell the story in my own words, and when I had finished sat thoughtfully staring into space.

The silence lengthened. I could feel myself trembling. At last I stole a look at his face. It was very angry.

'There is no need for me to tell you I hope, that you acted very wrongly, Miss

Lennox,' he began in a stern voice. 'This is purely a police matter. You should have come to me immediately that piece of evidence was found. I shall forbid Mr. McDonnell to enter the Francis' flat again. He has violated my trust in him.'

I hung my head and said miserably, 'I know it was wrong of us, but we so wanted to help.'

He softened slightly. 'You must leave these matters to us. I don't wish to be unkind, but warnings seem to have no effect upon you. You placed yourselves in grave danger. Mr. Roberts has, as it happens, told us of his misstatement, and that he did leave the club that night. But we are no further advanced. It has not assisted the case as yet.'

An idea had occurred to me while he was speaking.

'This accident,' I said slowly. 'I suppose it was an accident, not — ?'

Inspector Nevil eyed me severely. 'I think we can safely assume that the lorry which crashed into Mr. Roberts' car, did so accidentally. Don't let your imagination colour everything that happens, Miss

Lennox, or you will find yourself in more trouble.' He gave a little cough and rose to his feet.

'I must be going now. Thank you again for the coffee.' At the door, he paused and fixed me with a stern eye. 'No more investigating, Miss Lennox?'

'No more,' I promised solemnly, and satisfied, he went downstairs. I watched until the doors swung to behind him and he was gone.

★   ★   ★

At a quarter to one I phoned Stephen. He lunched after the office staff and this was the time to catch him.

'Rosemary!' he said, and I beamed as I heard the pleasure in his voice. 'My dear, I was just this minute going to call you. How about meeting me for lunch in half an hour?'

'Oh, that would be lovely, darling,' I cried eagerly. 'I'm so bored and it's ages since we had lunch together.'

'Well, make it at Robinson's. I'll meet you inside the entrance in half an hour then, darling. Goodbye.'

I scuttled back upstairs, and began a lightning transformation. When I reached Robinson's, I was five minutes late, but my morale, bolstered by sheer nylon and my best black suit, was high. Stephen was waiting patiently and his face lit up as I came towards him. 'Rosemary darling! The rest has done you good, you're looking a little better.'

This was not quite the greeting I had hoped for, but I felt his intentions were good, so I squeezed his arm, said how pleased I was to see him, and we went in.

Stephen has a gift for ordering food. Everything goes smoothly, there are no arguments, and the meal is always perfect. Over lunch we talked. There was so much to tell him, and he listened carefully as I poured out the story. 'I don't like the idea of you interfering like that, Rosemary,' he said finally. 'The Inspector is quite right.' Seeing he was taking it in that way, I cheerfully laid the blame at Bob's door and excused myself of any such intentions.

After this was settled, the conversation

took a more personal trend. We discussed my proposed stay at his home. It transpired that the weekend could not be managed, his Mother had relations staying so it was to be deferred a week. Fervently hoping that my relief was not too apparent. I proffered polite verbal messages to her and Stephen seemed quite happy. I too was content, feeling like the prisoner in the condemned cell who is suddenly granted a stay of execution.

The time went by all too quickly, and after a glance at the clock, we rose regretfully. I walked a little way with him and said goodbye at the corner. He arranged to ring me the next day and then hurried back to the office.

I went to the cinema. It was a beautiful afternoon, just right for a walk in the park, but I am not the athletic type and though it was a shocking waste of my best costume in I went!

It was a terrifying film! My evil star had led me to the cinema on the circuit showing a horror film!

The sensible thing to do in a case like that, is to leave and promptly, but I was held rivetted in my seat by a fascinated horror, and I saw it through. Needless to say, Rosemary Lennox was not her usual happy self as she walked out of the cinema!

All the shops were shut, so I made my way home. Elly was in now. I could hear her bustling about next door. She had company. A woman's laugh rose above the clatter, and I guessed it was one of Elly's relations.

My flat was in an awful mess. My housework had been very sketchy of late, and the whole place needed a thorough cleanup. I put away my finery and going to the opposite extreme, I dug out an old boiler suit and a sloppy Joe woolly. Thus attired, I went ahead like two women, sweeping and polishing every inch. I was rummaging energetically under the bed, when someone knocked on the door — Now, whoever could that be? Stephen would be home by now, and Bob was out. Muttering to myself I crawled out, straightened my back, which ached slightly, and marched, duster in hand, to the door.

It was Bob, after all. He grinned. A particularly aggravating grin. 'Doing some housework, Rosie?'

'Oh no,' I said sarcastically. 'I'm just off to a Ball at the Mansion House!'

'The Lord Mayor will be surprised,' he murmured and not waiting for an invitation, walked in. To be quite truthful, I was glad of the excuse to stop, and sank gratefully down on the settee.

'Not used to it, eh?' Bob chuckled. 'Now, now, don't show that nasty temper! Uncle Robert will make you some tea. Sit there like a good girl.'

Reclining my aching back against the cushions, I listened to the pleasing sound of the kettle being filled, and the clatter of cups. Soon he came in. 'Uncle Robert's cure for housewives. Never been known to fail!' he announced pushing a steaming cup towards me. Then lighting two cigarettes, and handing me one, he flopped into the chair opposite.

'I hear you met our friend the Inspector today.'

'Oh, has he phoned or something?'

'Not only the dread Inspector, but Old

Moneybags too! They've both been dinning the error of my ways to me.' I sat up at that and looked guilty. He shook his head sorrowfully. 'It appears I dragged the unwilling, protesting Miss Lennox into my schemes, when all she asked was a little peace!'

'Well!' I said weakly, 'you know what Stephen is. I had to say something.'

Bob laughed silently for a few minutes, then sobered a little. 'I was sorry to hear about Roberts. He's alright though I take it? What in the world made you go to the hospital, Rosie?'

'I don't know really, just felt sorry, I suppose.' I told him about the girl in the waiting room and he sighed thoughtfully. 'Well, it may work out, you can never tell.'

'It seems we're back where we started Bob. Our investigation didn't bear a lot of fruit, did it?'

'No — and the killer, whoever he is, is still at large — well, I'm off.'

'Where are you going?' I asked, startled by his abruptness.

'Freda's holding a little 'shindig' and I said I'd drop in. Bye Rosie. See you sometime.' Patting my head in a fatherly way, he strolled out.

This Freda of Bob's was figuring more and more often in his conversation lately. He always seemed to be meeting or phoning her. I'd tried to like the girl, but it was quite useless. The very mention of her name annoyed me. She was not the one for Bob.

A few minutes later, Elly knocked, and stood talking, admiring the results of all my hard toil. The flat certainly did look better. The floors and furniture shone, and the carpet was spotless. 'Very nice, dear,' she said approvingly. 'Did I hear Bob go downstairs just now?'

'Yes, he's gone out with Freda,' I replied. 'Did you want him?'

'Only to return his raincoat. He left it in my room the other day, and I've been meaning to give it back to him.'

'Oh, give it to me, Elly, I'll run up with it later, I can hang it on that fancy doorknocker he's fixed up.' We both laughed, Bob's doorknocker was a gruesome gargoyle. It had taken his eye and despite all opposition he'd nailed it firmly on the door. I took the coat, said goodnight, and went inside.

There were just a few things left to do, and I had cleared up, washed and put my pyjamas on, before I remembered Bob's coat again. It was a disreputable garment, the lining torn and two buttons missing from the front. Two buttons? A cold tremor ran through me, and I sat clasping the coat feeling strangely helpless. Yesterday I had held two buttons in my hand, when we were searching the Francis' flat. Bob had dismissed them contemptuously as probably belonging to John, and not thinking I'd slipped them in my pocket. Unwillingly I got up and went to the wardrobe. Yes, they were still in the pocket of my dress. My hand shaking, I compared them with the buttons on Bob's raincoat. They matched perfectly!

I sank down on the bed, my brain whirling. Piece by piece the evidence against him was growing. The blue matchbox, the man at the club who thought he'd seen him there a week ago. The swift assumption that Les Roberts was involved; and now this.

I must have sat there a long time, but at last wearily I took the raincoat back into the living room, and carefully sewed the missing buttons into position. Then I went upstairs to Bob's; flat, and hung it on the doorknocker!

In my room I tried to work things out. That Bob was involved in some way with the murders, I had now no doubt, but that he had actually committed them? No. My brain rejected the idea furiously. Bob was not a murderer. I would never believe it of him. Somewhere there was an explanation, if I could only see it.

But I couldn't see it. Over and over the details pounded in my head, until in desperation I flung myself down on the bed and beat at the pillow with my fists.

Not Bob — not Bob — it mustn't be.

Why not, a voice kept whispering. Why not? And at last, at long last I faced the truth. I wouldn't believe him guilty, because I didn't want to. Deep in my heart, behind all our arguing and quarrelling lay the truth unrealized till now. I was in love with Bob. I would fight desperately to save him.

Wave after wave of joy and exhilaration broke over me. In the midst of all the terror and doubt, I was suddenly wildly happy. Stephen and all I hoped to mean to him faded as if he never existed. There was no one in the world but Bob. It was Bob who had reached me first, that terrible night when I discovered Mary's body, and the comfort and safety of his arms had been indescribable. I remembered his words. 'You're safe now, darling. I'm here. I won't let anything hurt you,' and again the fierce rush of joy shook me. All through these terrible days he had been beside me, helping and reassuring. But after a few minutes, the doubts came back again, and I lay worrying far into the night.

7

Fearful discovery

The postman left two letters the next morning. One from Stephen saying he would not be able to see me over the weekend, as his Mother had booked seats for a show, and one from the office. A polite communication enclosing my pay slip and a frigid note to the effect, that they hoped I was better but my presence on Monday would naturally be expected.

Both left me quite cold. Stephen no longer occupied my thoughts. He seemed so unreal, and apart from the life I had been leading, and as for the office — I appreciated the money of course, but the sentiments were decidedly chilling!

Elly knocked a little later. 'Oh you're dressed,' she said in some surprise.

I laughed. My habits had become quite Bohemian during the last few days, and I felt rather ashamed. 'I must try to get back in training. It's work next week, you know. Are you going out so early?'

She sat down, carefully smoothing her skirt. 'I'm off to see my cousin at Pinner.'

'Again? You were there yesterday, weren't you?'

She nodded. 'Yes, it's a nuisance really. But she phoned up this morning and said her little boy was ill, and could I possibly come over for a bit.'

'And you said 'yes,' of course,' I scolded. 'Honestly Elly, people are inclined to take advantage of your kind heart. Don't you ever think of yourself?'

Elly chuckled. 'Oh, get along with you. There'll be time enough for that when I'm an old woman.'

'You never will be at this rate,' I nagged. But I might as well have talked to the armchairs. It was a waste of breath. When Elly hears of anyone in trouble, she always is the first on the doorstep.

We chatted a bit longer. 'Bob was in very late last night,' she said crossly. 'He woke me up slamming his door. I don't know what's the matter with him lately. He seems a changed man, worried and short-tempered. No time for anyone. The Inspector noticed it too.'

I drew a quick breath and said guardedly: 'Inspector Nevil?'

'Yes. You know he came round the other night. The night you two were out playing detectives. We kept going over things and he said Bob was acting strangely. I think he put it down to the fact that he was on the spot each time the murders were committed. He stressed the point repeatedly.'

I broke in quickly. 'Well, that's nothing — we were all there.'

'That's what I said, but he seemed more concerned about Bob, than you or I. Oh, it's all a lot of nonsense. I do believe that Inspector's trying to set us against one another. I don't know why I'm talking about it now, I should be on the bus by this time.' She gave me a parting kiss and hurried off downstairs.

I sat anxiously going over what she had said. Last night I had resolved to forget my suspicions, but Inspector Nevil was suspicious too. Things looked bad. Everything was mounting against Bob, and I could do nothing.

The details banged in my head, condemning him, but I thrust them aside angrily, refusing to listen.

A shout from the passage made my heart jump. It was Bob. A wild thrill of delight ran through me and gripping the table to steady myself, I called out as casually as I could manage, 'Coming.'

I was afraid to meet his eyes when I opened the door. Afraid that he would see, mirrored in them, the feelings I was fighting to control. The sight of him, the unruly black hair, the twinkling eyes, sent my blood racing gaily, and I wanted to shout my love aloud so that everyone should know. Instead with an effort, I managed to say calmly: 'Good morning, Bob. How was the party?'

He grinned excitedly. 'Very interesting, my poppet. You should have come along.'

I restrained myself from pointing out that neither he, nor that wretched Freda, had invited me and produced a sisterly smile.

'I came to thank you for mending my raincoat. It was very sweet of you. I think you're getting the motherly instinct at last!'

'How did you know it was me?' I stammered.

He laughed. 'Now let me think. I saw that it was mended. I examined the work closely, and asked myself a question. Who among my large circle of girl friends, would sew on grey buttons with pink cotton? Quick as a flash I got the answer. Rosie posie!'

'Oh, Bob!'

'Thank you all the same honey. It's the thought what counts! By the way I don't remember leaving my raincoat in your flat.'

'You didn't,' I said carefully. 'Elly found it on her chair, and gave it to me.'

'And didn't mend it? For shame! I shall have to speak to Elly, she's getting careless!'

My heart was beating fast now. 'She didn't know where the buttons were.'

'Oh,' he said in a humouring sort of voice. 'Where were they, under the bed?'

'They were in the Francis' flat.'

He stopped smiling then, and looked at

me in surprise. 'In the flat? What do you mean?'

Desperately, I went on. I had to know, to find out the truth. 'You remember, Bob, I found them that day we searched for evidence. You thought they were John's.'

He whistled softly. 'Did you by George!' I stood silent. Praying for him to say something that would explain and clear away the whole horrid episode. But he just whistled again and said rather thoughtfully. 'That's damned funny.'

We were both silent for a minute and then Bob began to chuckle. 'You're a very naughty girl, you know. You should have taken those buttons straight round to Inspector Nevil. He'll say it's another case of withholding evidence.'

I remained silent. He gave me a long enquiring look. 'Why didn't you, Rosie?' Still I kept quiet, but the colour rose in my cheeks. Bob watched me closely and his voice was strangely loud as he repeated the question. 'Why didn't you?'

I took a deep breath and managed to get out: 'I thought it might implicate you.'

'Implicate me?'

I could stand no more. My nerves already stretched to breaking point, snapped, and a torrent of words tumbled from my lips. 'He suspects you Bob! I'm sure of it. Elly let something slip this morning. You must get away, they'll trap you — ' My voice rose hysterically and I broke off, shivering and trembling.

He gripped my arms tightly and glanced along the passage, pushed me into the room, kicking the door shut, behind us. I collapsed into a chair and buried my face in my hands, vainly trying to pull myself together.

Bob stood a little back from me. For a few seconds he said nothing, then quickly he began to talk, his voice soothing. 'Now listen to me, Rosemary, you've reached the state when everything seems to be piling up. You're nervy and unstrung. It's understandable after all you've been through. But there isn't a scrap of evidence against me,' his voice sharpened. 'Good God! You don't think I killed them do you?'

I opened my mouth to tell him about

the matchbox, the man at the club, all the little things that I had compiled so painfully, but something stopped me, and I just shook my head.

He gave me a worried glance, and coming over stroked my hair. 'Don't worry me any more, my sweet. There's some explanation for those wretched buttons. I tell you what. When I get home tonight, we'll talk the whole thing over and try to put your mind at rest. I've got to go now. I'm late already. Are you alright now?'

'Yes, Bob. I was silly.'

'I'll see you later then, about half past seven.'

I cleared up the breakfast things, put on my hat and coat and went out. To have stayed alone in my flat doing nothing would have driven me crazy. It was a miserable day. Cold and misty, but I shopped and talked to people, deliberately spinning out the time. The gossip about John and Mary seemed to have died down, and I was thankful for that at least.

By twelve o'clock, my acquaintances

had all disappeared. I had no further excuse for shopping, so in desperation, I went to the café for lunch. The meal finished, I sat over my coffee for as long as I dared, but the increasing queue of people, waiting to be served, finally drove me out.

There was nothing else to do. I had to go back. Feeling utterly wretched, I walked along towards the flats. As I turned the corner, I was surprised to see a large car, standing outside. Curiously I quickened my pace, and pushing through the swing door, was brought to a sudden standstill. A man and woman were just coming out of the Francis flat.

For a second, the three of us stood staring at each other. Then the woman came across the hall towards me, smiling pleasantly. She was fair-haired, very slight and wore a pretty grey coat belted tightly at the waist.

'I wonder if you can help us,' she began. 'My name is Morely, Mrs. Catherine Morely, and this is my brother. The police gave us permission to come and collect poor Mary's things. Mrs.

Francis was my cousin. Perhaps you have heard her talk of me?'

I remembered the name. Mary had often mentioned her cousins, I believe she had said they lived in the country. I hastened to reply and asked if there was anything I could do.

'Thank you, we should be glad of your assistance. Oh, by the way, the police gave us a signed authority. Would you like to see it?' she queried, and produced a slip of paper from her pocket. I glanced at it quickly and saw that it was in order.

'What is it you want?' I asked.

'Well, we've brought a couple of cases along, but there's so much to clear, that they're quite full already. We're only halfway through too. If you have any boxes or carrier bags, anything like that, it would be such a help. It's not a very pleasant task, but as we're her only relations — anyway we'd rather not come back again. It's all very difficult.'

I could understand her feelings and after promising to see what I had in my flat, I hurried upstairs. A prolonged search revealed one carrier bag and an old shoebox, neither of which would be of much help. I was sorting through the kitchen cupboard again, when a sudden thought struck me. Elly always hoarded paper and boxes in the firm belief that they would always come in handy some time. If only she was in — I had the key to her flat somewhere. Months ago when she had caught a bad dose of influenza, I had been given a spare key, so that I could pop in and out without disturbing her. It was in the table drawer, tucked in paper. I felt sure Elly would not mind if I looked around her place. She was always the first to offer assistance, so I let myself in and started searching.

Sure enough, I found a whole selection of boxes, papers and carriers, neatly stored behind a curtain.

I staggered downstairs with the loot and Mrs. Morely clapped her hands. 'Oh, that's splendid. How very kind of you. Miss — ' she smiled enquiringly. 'I don't know your name, do I?'

'Miss Lennox. Rosemary Lennox.'

She nodded. 'Lennox. It seems familiar somehow — Oh my dear, you're the girl who found Mary.'

I shivered involuntarily and said yes, I was the girl. We didn't say much more, and I went back upstairs half sad, half relieved to think that now there would be nothing. Memories are not so easily forgotten.

The time passed slowly; I tidied up and put away the shopping. The grocer had been very generous. Tucked away among my purchases were two tins of steak, and on a sudden wave of energy, I started cooking. With complete recklessness, I opened both tins and made two large pies. Bob would need something to eat if he came straight home and Elly could have the other one. It was a change for me to cook her a dinner, but I knew she'd be pleased after being out all day. They came out of the oven nicely browned and quite professional and I was delighted with my efforts. By the time I had finished it was gone six.

Picking up Elly's key, I let myself into her flat again, gingerly carrying the pie. I couldn't decide whether to leave it in the kitchen or on the living room table, and while I was deliberating, my eye caught by the half open bedroom door. The bed was unmade.

Elly must have left in a real hurry. She hated having her home untidy. 'I'll make it up for her,' I muttered and switching on the light went in. The curtains too were still closed, an unbelievable laxity in one so precise as Elly.

I turned my attention to the bed, stripping it and plumping up the pillows, and as I reached for the blanket, I twisted, knocking something off the dressing table. Straightening up, I examined my find curiously.

It was a long glistening earring, fashioned from tiny pearls. I couldn't resist a smile as I laid it beside its fellow, somehow I had never associated Elly with glamorous jewellery. But apparently that was a mistake, for there was quite a lot of it heaped on the little gilt tray.

Wonderingly I dangled a jade necklet and its matching clip. They were lovely and vaguely, yes, vaguely familiar. Somewhere, not so long ago, I had seen this jade set. I shut my eyes and thought hard, trying to remember back. Gradually it came.

A girl in a gold dress. A girl who smiled at me from the foot of the stairs. The hall light had shone highlighting the necklet and her long blonde hair against the dark background. Long hair, that shimmered and fell in a golden cascade to her shoulders — The jade set fell to the ground with a clatter as my fingers went suddenly numb. Horrified I recoiled from that dressing table. It was Mary Francis' jewellery!

For a second, I couldn't realize what it meant. Stupidly I gazed round the room. It all looked so ordinary. Elly's dressing gown lay on the chair, warm and old-fashioned. On the rug, her cosy rather shabby slippers. The big wardrobe and chest of drawers. Everything so familiar and comforting. Yet there, on the dressing table was Mary's stolen jewellery.

My knees gave way abruptly, and I sank down on to the bed, trying to think clearly, Was I going mad or something? This morning I had suspected Bob. Now it was Elly. Elly whom I knew and loved so well. I must be out of my mind.

The jewellery had been missed immediately. Elly herself had seized on it as the reason for the murder. I remember her angry voice saying how foolish the police were not to follow it up more quickly. Yet while they had searched and sent out descriptions, all the time she had known it was here. A swift vision of her, sitting at the dressing table, playing with the jewels, crossed my mind, and I felt a sudden chill.

On impulse I got up and opened her wardrobe door. Mary's lace housecoat was also missing. If the jewels were here, the housecoat should be too. Unwillingly, I pushed among the sturdy tweeds and woollens, until my hand touched something soft at the very back. I pulled it out. It was the pink lace housecoat. The sleeves were torn and the seams gaped, as if someone too big had tried to squeeze into it.

I knew then. Whatever Elly might say, whatever explanation she could give, I knew, as surely as if I had been in the room with them, that it was she who had strangled Mary.

Standing by the big wardrobe, the housecoat clutched nervously in my hands, I faced the terrifying realization. To think that I of all people should make this fearful discovery. Elly and I had been so close. She had mothered and spoiled me in everything; I relied on her. Yet for the past week, with no sign, no alteration in her manner, she had kept her dreadful secret hidden.

Engrossed in my thoughts I stood motionless lost to the outer world. My dazed brain groping in darkness, knowing, but scarcely crediting what it must face. How long I stood there, I don't know, but a slight sound, the merest whisper of noise, suddenly froze my heart. With a terror that no words can describe, I realized that someone else was in the room with me! I turned my head slowly. There in the doorway, a strange smile playing about her lips, stood Elly.

8

Jealousy

I think that moment nearly turned my brain. I stared at Elly's motherly form, and for the first time I saw the strength in it. The sturdy legs planted so firmly. The thick body, powerful arms and shoulders. I raised my eyes to her face. It was evil. A cloak seemed to have dropped from it, and with a shudder I hid my face in my hands.

She laughed then. I pray God that I may never hear such laughter again. From a deep throaty chuckle it rose to maniacal shrillness, and when she stopped the echo of it hung in the air about us.

Leaning back against the door she watched me, warily and yet confidently. At last she spoke, and even her voice was changed.

'So you're still playing detectives, eh my dear? But this time you've really found something, haven't you? How did you get in here?'

She rapped the last question out, and I found myself answering like a guilty child, caught in some misdemeanour.

'Mary's cousin came to take away her things She asked for some carriers or boxes. I remembered that you always kept them and let myself in with the key you gave me a few months ago.'

She brooded over that for a bit, and said thoughtfully, 'I forgot about the key.'

'Elly,' I began desperately. She smiled, and keeping her eyes on me, half turned and locked the door, slipping the key into her pocket. 'It's no good doing that,' I said with a bravery I was far from feeling. 'I'll have to tell the police.'

At the word her face changed. An ugly expression showed in her eyes and coming swiftly forward she hit me across the mouth, knocking me back onto the bed.

'The police!' she spat. 'Those idiots! You'll tell them nothing. Nothing, do you hear?'

I lay looking up at her in terror, as she towered above me. Her ring had cut my cheek, and I could feel the warm blood trickling down my face. Suddenly she began to chuckle and rock backwards and forwards.

'John wanted to tell the police. I told him everything before I turned on the gas. He couldn't move then, the drug had got him, but he could still hear.'

I moved a little on the bed and she menaced me with her hands so that I lay still, hardly daring to breathe.

'No my dear,' she muttered softly. 'Oh, no. You've meddled once too often. There's no getting away with it this time. There'll be another body to puzzle the police.'

Terror gave me sudden strength and I sat up, defying her. 'Elly, you're sick. Only let me get you to a doctor. You don't know what you're doing.'

She chuckled again. 'Think I'm mad do you? Well, you're wrong my little Rosemary. I'm not mad. Who'd suspect old Elly? What possible motive could she have? Why, everyone knows what good friends we are.'

'Elly,' I gasped. 'If I found out, someone else will, it's — '

She cut me short abruptly. 'You're the only one who knows. So you must go. I've always hated you anyway, with your silly talk.' She primmed up her mouth in mockery *'Dear Elly. What should I do without you, you're like a mother to me! God how I've laughed.'*

I held my hands tightly together to stop them shaking. I knew I would need every ounce of strength and guile I possessed if I was ever to get out of here alive. My only hope was Bob. He had promised to look in tonight. It was about half past six now. If I could only keep her talking until I heard him knock on my door.

My lips were dry and I moistened them. Elly noticed the action and laughed, gloatingly.

'That's what Mary did. The little fool! So frightened she was.'

'Why did you kill her?'

'I didn't intend to, you know. I just wanted to talk to her. Hear about the quarrel. After you'd gone out I went down stairs with some cakes. She let me in and we talked for a bit. I could see she was restless so I asked her — I'd heard

John slam the door a while back. She flared up and told me to mind my own business, to get out of her flat, called me an old busybody. I decided to kill her then — just like that! She must have sensed it, because she suddenly stopped shouting and looked frightened.'

Elly paused and I saw that she was reliving the scene, word for word.

'I caught hold of her long yellow hair, and pulled her right close to my face. I told her how I'd always hated her stuck up ways and silly smile. Oh she was frightened! She looked ugly, like a rabbit with her hair pulled back. Her mouth was open and her neck was there close to my hands. I squeezed and squeezed and all the time I watched her face. She died looking into my eyes.'

I felt I must faint. The awful horror of that description, her eager excited voice as she dwelt on the details, all combined, and I felt the room begin to spin. Somehow I controlled the nausea that gripped me and listened as she continued.

'I let her drop to the floor. I wasn't sorry or frightened, I was glad — glad.

For the first time I knew my power. Then I thought what I must do next. Wipe away any fingerprints, take back the cakes. I looked all round the room and then I thought it would look better if something was stolen. So I went in to the bedroom and picked out the jewellery. That's when I saw the housecoat, so soft and pretty. I took that too. I carried her body into the bedroom and left the light and radio on. Then I went back to my flat. Everyone was out and nobody saw me in the fog as I left afterwards to meet my cousin for supper. It was all so easy.'

'The door,' I began, and she took the point up quickly.

'I thought it would be best if you found her. I knew what you'd do, you see! After I heard Bob come in I slipped downstairs and opened it. I'd taken the key away already. I was at the top of the stairs when you screamed, but stood back to let Bob and the others reach you first.

'It was so exciting,' she went on. 'Like acting in a play. Only I was directing as well as acting. That night when the police came to my room, and then John's, I thought I must laugh aloud when they took him to the station. And you! — ' She laughed shrilly. 'Sleeping in dear Elly's bed because you were afraid to sleep alone!'

I thought of that night when I had nestled up to Elly's warm back and felt so safe and secure. If I had known then! But I must keep her talking.

'What about John?' I asked in a voice that for all my resolve wavered slightly. 'You didn't hate him.'

'I hated them both!' she hissed fiercely. 'He made it so simple for me. The police already suspected him, and when you told me over the phone that he was coming back, I knew my opportunity was at hand. I didn't realize they'd be able to tell about the drug. Not that it made any difference, just mystified them more. I waited for him to go into the flat then I made a cup of coffee and added the laudanum.'

She smiled to herself and I glanced furtively at the clock. A quarter to seven, would Bob never come?

'He was so pleased. I kept my face away from him while he drank it, in case he should see my eyes and suspect. When he had finished he sat down and said he was feeling tired. I persuaded him to go into the bedroom and rest in the armchair. The poor fool did just what I suggested. Once he was well under the drug's hold I told him! Yes, I told him everything. I'll never forget his face. He struggled to reach me, but he was too weak. I watched him for a bit, then I turned on the gas and left him.'

Her cold brutality was worse even than the gloating enjoyment she had evinced when describing Mary's death. I stared at her, fascinated in spite of myself. She took her outdoor clothes and reaching down, snatched the pink housecoat that I still clutched in my trembling hands. Ignoring me she struggled into it, went over to the dressing table and selecting the glittering pearl earrings, screwed them on carefully.

Slowly she turned around, arms extended to show her glory. An insane desire to laugh ran through me as her squat powerful figure revolved in a grotesque display, but I saw my cue and grabbed it.

'Earrings suit you Elly.'

The praise had an amazing effect. Her hardness left her and she smiled shyly, like a girl. Fingering the dangling jewels, she murmured to herself.

'I always wanted pretty things, but we were too poor. Once my Aunt gave me an old row of beads. Blue they were. The clasp was broken but I re-threaded them and tied them on with ribbon.'

'You never had any others?' I asked playing desperately for time. She shook her head and the harsh look came back.

'They put me out to service, and from then on it was uniform and black stockings. No pretty things for Elly — she was too old, too plain. Keep them for the youngsters! Flashy blondes like Mary Francis. No brains but pretty faces.' She paused for breath, her eyes glaring.

'Elly,' I said hastily. 'Try the jade bracelet on.' She turned back to the dressing table obediently, and I felt a little safer.

I must get to my feet while she was occupied. Stealthily I stood up and took a hesitant careful step. It was a mistake.

And that moment she swung round, a brush gripped m her hand. I held my breath and stayed where I was.

'I know what you're trying to do,' she hissed. 'You think you'll get away while I'm not looking. But you won't my girl. You know my secret. You've got to die like the others.'

We faced each other across that little space. The blood was drumming in my ears, my body was tense, waiting. Suddenly with no warning she sprang at, me flinging the brush aside, her big hands groping for my throat. Her weight carried me back against the bed, and we fell on it struggling desperately.

Somehow I writhed away and ran to the door, beating on it and screaming in wild terror. In a second she was there. Her hand gripped my throat and I heard her animal grunt of satisfaction. I tore at that grinning, sweating face. Choking and sobbing, my breath coming in painful harsh jerks, I fought for life. But she was too strong for me.

The room began to go black. There was a grinding roar in my ears and just as I felt consciousness slipping from me, the pressure by a miracle ceased.

I slumped to the floor. Far away voices were raised, someone was banging on the door. I heard it all in a daze, but I could do nothing to help myself. My strength was exhausted. Elly stood over me panting and glaring at the door. Muttering unintelligibly she ran to the fireplace and dragging the heavy old-fashioned fire irons from their box, braced herself defiantly.

The next minute, the panels splintered like matchwood round the lock, the door caved inwards, and Bob, Inspector Nevil and two or three policemen hurled themselves into the room. Elly backed at the sudden onslaught, mouthing silently. Bob picked me up, heedless of her and the others and I saw as in a dream that he was shaking and sweating.

'Thank God you're alive,' he gasped. 'I thought we were too late.'

Inspector Nevil's voice cut in. It was a hard merciless voice. 'Ellen Moreland,' he began, 'I arrest — ' But we heard no more. A wild scream of rage rent the air. The men in the doorway ducked instinctively as Elly, her face contorted, flung the heavy fire irons at them, and ran to the window.

'Stop her!' yelled the Inspector. 'She's going to jump! Stop her!'

But they were too late. There was a crash of breaking glass, a shrill cackle and she was gone.

Bob had hidden my face against his coat, and mercifully I did not see that last desperate leap. To hear it was enough. Everything, the fear and horror of the scene, combined in that awful minute. I screamed once and then knew no more.

★　★　★

When I opened my eyes I was lying on my bed, back in my own flat. A strange man bent over me and touched my head with gentle hands. He smiled kindly.

'That's better Miss Lennox. You had us worried for a bit. Now don't try to sit up, just lay there and rest.'

'I'm all right,' I started, 'a bit shaken that's all.'

'Of course,' he soothed. 'Drink this first

and then you can talk.' He held a glass of milky fluid to my lips. It had a bitter taste, and my throat was stiff and painful but I drank it obediently, then lay back against the pillows.

From the street below, a buzz of voices rose through the window. Two policemen were bustling about the room, and there at the foot of my bed stood Bob and Inspector Nevil. For a moment I gazed at them blankly and then tears, that I was unable to control, flooded my cheeks.

Bob was at my side in a second. 'Easy now darling,' he said softly. 'It's all over. No one can hurt you.' He patted my eyes with his big handkerchief and went on talking calmly and steadying me until I was able to sit up and produce a faint watery smile.

Inspector Nevil came over beaming and rubbing his hands. 'As Mr. McDonnell says it's all over, my dear. You mustn't upset yourself any more.' The wail of a departing ambulance siren suddenly split the air and another policeman appeared in the doorway to murmur something to the Inspector.

'Yes, very well. Get that crowd cleared away down there and then get back to the station. I'll see the rest of you there later. Oh, Johnson, I shall need you. Got your notes? Right!'

The two policemen and the doctor went, leaving Bob, Inspector Nevil, the dour Johnson and myself. Johnson shut the door, pulled out his notebook and gazed at me expectantly. The Inspector sat down and offered his cigarettes round. He lit mine and I drew on it deeply. I was feeling steadier every minute. Steady enough to put the question I had been afraid to ask as yet.

'Is she — is she dead, Bob?'

He nodded grimly but said nothing as I took a deep shuddering breath of relief.

Inspector Nevil cleared his throat and gave me a kindly smile. 'Now Miss Lennox, I'm afraid I'm going to start asking questions again, but if you don't feel up to it, say so, and we'll leave it till later.' He looked enquiringly at me, his head cocked on one side. My little birdman, I thought affectionately, replying that I'd rather get it over and be done.

He nodded his satisfaction.

As it happened there were very few questions. He let me tell my story without interruption and when I reached the part about banging on the door and hearing their voices, he patted my shoulder kindly. Choking back my rising hysteria I glanced at Bob, he was listening intently and as I stopped speaking, said in a low voice, 'She was mad of course. Raving mad!'

'I wouldn't say that,' the Inspector returned thoughtfully. 'She was a bitterly jealous woman: That jealousy warped her brain and made her secretly hate anything young or pretty but she controlled it. Perhaps at the last she was mad, but the underlying evil in her nature drove her to commit those two murders, and attempted a third. I am convinced she was as sane as you or I at the time.'

I put a question that had been puzzling me. 'How was it that you all arrived together like that? Did somebody hear me and call the police?'

Bob answered, smiling a little. 'Well it was all your fault Rosie.' He laughed at my surprised face. 'This morning you worried me stiff about those damned buttons. I could see you were at the end of your tether, and certainly it did look suspicions as far as I was concerned. Anyway I puzzled all day over it, trying to think how the devil my buttons could be in the Francis' flat, until I was nearly off my head. I decided the only thing to do was to get in touch with the Inspector here.'

Inspector Nevil took up the tale. 'It was the first wise move anyone made in this case and I welcomed Mr. McDonnell's co-operation. We thrashed it out bit by bit. Going over every little fact until emerging quite clear from all our discussions was an astonishing theory.

'Everything came back to Ellen Moreland. She had what everybody else lacked. The opportunity. Each time the lock had been intact on the door of the Francis' flat, proving that both victims had opened it willingly to let in someone they knew and trusted. Each time Ellen Moreland had known they were alone, and had as we realized at last, an unsubstantiated alibi for the actual time of death. The cinema — shopping — her mention of people met during these expeditions had misled us, she could quite easily have been in the flats, and who was more trusted? That open door now. That always worried me. Why should Miss Lennox find it open within a few minutes of Mr. McDonnell and Ellen Moreland insisting it was shut? Someone had obviously slipped down and opened it between those times. Again, she had the opportunity.'

'But how did you work all that out from Bob's two buttons?' I asked, mystified.

'Quite easily. You see they weren't his!'

'Not his?' I cried. 'Why, they matched perfectly.'

'No, they were not a perfect match. Very near, and to one in your excited condition, the same, but nevertheless not the right buttons.'

'But he had two missing from his raincoat and I naturally thought — '

'You thought what you were intended to think. The previous day you had told Ellen Moreland everything about your search. You gave her an idea. Mr. McDonnell's raincoat was in her possession. She ripped off the two buttons, guessing that the difference would be negligible, and discussed the coat with you. Quite naturally to save her trouble you offered to return it. She probably waited, then crept upstairs to examine it after you were in bed. She completed the good work this morning by hinting that the police suspected Mr. McDonnell of being involved and then left the next move to you.'

'And I made it!' I sighed ruefully.

'It was the most fortunate thing you could have done, as things turned out. Once Mr. McDonnell and I had established the fact that the coat had been in Ellen Moreland's possession since the murders were committed and that the buttons did not belong, everything began to fall into place. Naturally we had no proof. I doubt very much if we could have discountenanced her on a flimsy piece of guesswork like that. Still, the implications were too serious to ignore, and in my own mind I was convinced. There and then we began to feel a great anxiety for you Miss Lennox.'

He gave me a quick friendly glance and went on, 'My intentions were to persuade you to leave home for a while. You were in grave danger I felt, but as we turned in at the door we heard you scream — ' He shook his head thoughtfully. 'That was a very bad moment.'

Bob lit another cigarette and said feelingly, 'Thank God we were in time. Any delay, a moment's hesitation, and it would have been too late.'

I shivered. 'Don't, Bob.'

Inspector Nevil patted my arm. 'It's over now, you must try not to think back.' He gave a little cough. 'I think that clears everything up satisfactorily. You and Mr. McDonnell will of course have to put in an appearance at the inquest, but we'll try to keep it out of the papers as much as possible. I shall want you both in my office tomorrow morning to settle the final details. About eleven shall we say?'

Bob and I agreed to this, and he rose to go. I tried, very poorly I'm afraid, to express all the gratitude I felt. He hushed me quickly, refusing to listen. 'I'm only thankful that we were able to be of some use at the moment. Goodnight Miss Lennox. The doctor left these tablets. He wants you to take two tonight. They'll help you sleep.' He smiled kindly in parting. 'Tomorrow everything will seem different Miss Lennox. Again. Good-night.'

He closed the door leaving Bob and I alone. I turned to him eagerly, but before I could say a word there was another knock at the door. Bob answered it. Johnson's massive form loomed up.

'Excuse me Sir, but there's a young man down here asking for Miss Lennox. Says his name's Stephen Lane.'

Bob called out, 'It's Stephen, do you want to see him?'

I didn't. All I wanted was to be alone with Bob, but I could hardly say so. 'I suppose you'd better tell him to come up,' I said rather ungraciously.

He came back into the bedroom. I felt his eyes rest on me questioningly but I said nothing and soon Stephen joined us.

Stephen was worried and anxious. He

had met Inspector Nevil downstairs and heard a brief outline of everything that had happened. Now his one concern was to get me to his mother's.

'But you're all fixed up Stephen,' I protested weakly.

'My dear Rosemary, I can't allow you to stop here alone. We'll think of something,' he insisted, brushing this aside.

Suddenly everything was too much for me. I didn't want to go or be argued about. All I wanted was a little peace. Stupidly and for no real reason I began to cry. Bob and Stephen looked at me helplessly.

It was Bob who settled the matter. 'Look here, I think she'll be just as well off in her own flat as with strangers. I'll get someone to stay with her and later, when she's stronger, she can come to you.' There was a lot more arguing, during which Bob slipped out to the phone.

'It's all fixed,' he announced on his return. 'A friend of mine, Freda Ellis, is coming. Rosemary knows her, don't you pet? She'll be here in ten minutes.'

I sobbed even louder at this, but no one luckily knew my feelings towards Freda and it passed unnoticed. Stephen and Bob sat talking quietly, while I lay back in my bed. I kept my eyes shut, but I was acutely aware of them. I supposed I would marry Stephen in the end, and Bob would marry his wretched Freda never knowing how much I loved him. The tears began to trickle down my cheeks again at this thought and Stephen came over to comfort me. An ironic situation.

Freda Ellis arrived a few minutes later, breathless and clasping a weekend case in her hand. She and Bob murmured together at the door and I tried shamelessly to hear what they said. I caught Bob's murmured ' — completely unstrung, reaction of course — ' and her soft ' — poor kid, leave her to me — ' but I missed the rest. After a bit the men withdrew tactfully and I was left alone with Freda. I stared defiantly, determined to be difficult.

She made it very hard for me. Instead

of the gentle sympathy I expected, she bustled round preparing a meal, ignoring my protestation that I couldn't touch anything. Before I knew where I was she had me sitting in the kitchen, cautiously swallowing a little piece of my pie. To my surprise I found I was hungry. The stiffness had gone from my throat.

Freda smiled. 'Nice cooking Rosemary. Somebody's going to be a lucky husband.'

I flushed and said awkwardly, 'I'm glad you like it.'

She laughed teasingly. 'No need to be shy with me. I suppose it was that good looking man who was here when I arrived.' Not waiting for a reply she continued cheerfully, 'If you get tired of him, let me know! He's too nice for general circulation and I'm all ready to be swept off my feet.'

I kept my eyes down. 'I thought you had Bob all lined up.'

Freda shook her head and poured out the tea expertly. 'No, I'm not Bob's type, worse luck. We're just friends.'

Accepting the proffered cup, I sipped it thoughtfully and said with elaborate casualness, 'I wonder what his type is?'

She glanced at me. 'Who knows? He'll fall when the right girl comes along, they all do. Anyway, what are we doing wasting our time discussing men. I promised those two gadabouts that I'd have you tucked up in bed by nine o'clock, and it's half past already. They'll give me a bad reference.'

Thus admonished, I finished my tea and obediently swallowed two of the doctor's tablets. Freda had run my bath, scenting it liberally with bathsalts, and I relaxed in it thankfully. I could hear her singing gaily in the kitchen as she cleared away the things. Since our conversation I wondered why I had ever disliked this girl who was so sweet and kind.

She wanted to sleep on the couch but I wouldn't allow that. My bed was pretty roomy so in the end we shared it. The tablets were strong. My head seemed barely to touch the pillow before I was asleep, and knew no more until the morning.

The sound of the curtains being drawn back awakened me at last. I turned over, stretching blissfully, and Freda smiled down at me. 'Morning, Rosemary.'

I smiled back. 'Morning, Freda. Oh, how lovely. The sun's shining.'

She handed me my dressing gown. 'Up you get sleepy head. It's ten o'clock and breakfast awaits you.'

I scrambled out of bed. Yesterday's horror seemed like a bad dream in the bright sunlight. For the first time in days I felt safe and normal.

Freda was sitting at the table wearing one of my aprons. 'No need to ask if you slept well,' she chuckled. 'You look a different person.'

'I feel different. I can never thank you enough for being so kind last night. I was just about ready to give up.'

'You've been through a terrible experience, Rosemary,' she said seriously. 'I'm only too glad Bob called me, so skip the thanks and let's forget it. Eh? Now, breakfast.'

Bob had arranged to pick me up at a quarter to eleven, and I was ready and waiting at twenty to. It wasn't going to be a very pleasant morning, but the thought of seeing him again filled me with a bubbling happiness that nothing could suppress.

Freda answered his knock and I turned to greet him, my heart thumping so loudly I was convinced he must hear it.

'Hello Rosie, feeling better?' he asked.

'Fine thanks,' I returned. 'Are you ready to see Inspector Nevil?'

'I certainly am,' he said cheerfully. 'Never thought I'd go to a police station so willingly. Has she been a good girl, Freda?'

Freda nodded. She had watched me closely since Bob came into the room, her eyes understanding. 'Yes, an excellent patient. Come on now, it doesn't do to keep the police waiting. I'll see you in a moment.' At the door she squeezed my arm and gave me such a saucy look that the hot colour dyed my cheeks, and I ran after Bob blushing like a schoolgirl.

Inspector Nevil welcomed us kindly into his official looking room. After everything was dictated and signed legally, we sat chatting for a while.

'I see the papers are playing it down

Sir,' Bob said, stretching his long legs towards the gas fire.

'Yes they've co-operated well. We shall be able to bring in a verdict of unsound mind at the inquest I trust, and so let the whole matter die away. There's been too much publicity altogether. I'm sure you've both experienced it.'

He bent towards me. 'I'm glad to see you looking so much better Miss Lennox. None the worse for your frightening experience, I hope?'

'Oh no,' I replied eagerly. 'I'm just thankful it's all over. I'm not going to think about it any more.'

He nodded. 'Going down to your young man's home for a rest, I believe. Do you good, to get away from everything for a while.'

I let this pass. To tell the truth I hadn't given it a thought since last night. Stephen deserved a wife who loved him. Not one whose heart was with someone else. Perhaps he would marry his Shelia, the girl who always popped in and out. His mother would certainly approve of that match.

We talked a bit longer and finally rose to take our leave. It seemed strange to think that apart from the inquest, this was probably the last time we should see the Inspector. He had become such a familiar figure in our lives. We said goodbye, shook hands and left him to yet another case.

Outside the sun was shining in all its glory. It was such a lovely morning. One of those rare days that come to cheer us, with the promise of Spring ahead. 'Let's walk through the park,' Bob suggested. 'We can get a coffee at that little place in Kensington.' He tucked my arm in his and we set out, walking briskly.

I tripped along by his side, glowing with happiness. Darling, darling, darling went my heart. The awful suspicion and my fears for him were gone. I could have laughed aloud from sheer joy. He was the first to speak. 'When are you going down to Stephen's?' he inquired.

I came back to earth with a bump and earnestly wished the Inspector to the nether region for mentioning the subject. 'I'm not,' I said flatly. It was a relief to say it and make the decision.

'Why not?'

'I don't want to.'

'Why?'

This was getting a little out of hand and I made no reply. 'Why don't you want to go?' Bob repeated clearly.

'Oh for goodness sake, stop asking questions Bob. I'm not going and that's an end to it.'

We had left the park and were walking along the tree-lined avenue leading to the Serpentine. We continued in silence for a while. 'Freda's an awfully nice girl,' I said carefully.

He grinned. 'I'll bet you women have been gossiping about Stephen and myself. My ears burned all last night.'

This was a little too near the mark, but I couldn't resist the subject. 'I suppose you two will be settling down one day?'

He shrugged. 'I suppose so, but not with each other.'

'Oh,' I said, trying to quell the rush of exhilaration this plain statement gave me.

'How about you and Stephen?'

'Nothing like that about us,' I lied cheerfully. 'We're just good friends.'

There was another silence.

'Rosie?'

'Yes Bob?'

'Why did you upset yourself, and not inform the police about those buttons and everything else you'd cooked up against me?'

I nearly walked into the Serpentine at that one. Frantically I racked my brains for a plausible answer but none came.

Bob stopped walking. Putting his hand under my chin he tilted my face up to his. For a long breathless moment we looked at each other. His eyes were very gentle, but behind was the wicked glint I knew so well. I caught my breath as an unbelievable hope assailed me.

'Remember that evening, when you thought I was Stephen, and I kissed you?'

'Yes, Bob.' My heart thudded violently now.

He looked at me quizzically. 'I'd like to do it again but you made such a scene last time. I'm half afraid to.'

If I'd been in my right senses, I could have made some witty casual reply, but I was far removed from all sense. I was bouncing joyously on a pink-edged cloud and witty remarks had nothing to do with my feelings. In a small voice I answered meekly: 'I wouldn't make a scene, Bob.'

He pulled me to him. His strong arms came round me and for a dizzy wonderful moment we clung together. 'Darling,' he gasped shakily. 'Oh, darling I love you.'

I touched his cheek with a trembling hand 'And I love you Bob, so much.' He kissed me again, a long passionate kiss.

People were passing giving us amused, rather startled glances, but little we cared. The trees had suddenly burst into blossom, a heavy perfume hung in the air, and all the church bells in London seemed to ring gaily for us. At last I knew what love was.

Bob leaned back against a tree, rumpling my curls, and laughing a little. 'We had to come to it, Rosie. I think I must have loved you from the first moment I saw your impudent red head peeping round the door.'

'It was the same with me, darling — but we argued and wrangled so, I never realized it. Oh dear, what a lot of

180

time we've wasted.'

His eyes glinted wickedly. 'Let's not waste any more.'

Twisting imaginary whiskers he made a theatrical plunge at me, I side stepped, and ran laughing through the trees until he caught me. 'Rosie Lennox,' he said severely. 'If this is how you treat me now, what will it be like when we're married?'

Delirious with happiness I could only cling to him. I knew what life was going to be from now on. Wonderful!

CLIMATE INCORPORATED
THE FIVE MATCHBOXES
EXCEPT FOR ONE THING
BLACK MARIA, M.A.
ONE STEP TOO FAR
THE THIRTY-FIRST OF JUNE
THE FROZEN LIMIT
ONE REMAINED SEATED
THE MURDERED SCHOOLGIRL
SECRET OF THE RING
OTHER EYES WATCHING
I SPY . . .
FOOL'S PARADISE
DON'T TOUCH ME
THE FOURTH DOOR
THE SPIKED BOY
THE SLITHERERS
MAN OF TWO WORLDS
THE ATLANTIC TUNNEL
THE EMPTY COFFINS
LIQUID DEATH
PATTERN OF MURDER
NEBULA
THE LIE DESTROYER
PRISONER OF TIME

We do hope that you have enjoyed reading this large print book.

Did you know that all of our titles are available for purchase?

We publish a wide range of high quality large print books including:
Romances, Mysteries, Classics
General Fiction
Non Fiction and Westerns

Special interest titles available in large print are:
The Little Oxford Dictionary
Music Book, Song Book
Hymn Book, Service Book

Also available from us courtesy of Oxford University Press:
Young Readers' Dictionary
(large print edition)
Young Readers' Thesaurus
(large print edition)

For further information or a free brochure, please contact us at:
Ulverscroft Large Print Books Ltd.,
The Green, Bradgate Road, Anstey,
Leicester, LE7 7FU, England.
Tel: (00 44) **0116 236 4325**
Fax: (00 44) **0116 234 0205**

Other titles in the
Linford Mystery Library:

DEATH ASKS THE QUESTION

John Russell Fearn

Seemingly grand from the outside, the interior of Abner Hilton's house was a dilapidated, gloomy place — reflecting its morbid and desperately impoverished occupant. But Hilton's insane plan would lift him out of his poverty. He would murder his young niece, who was about to visit him; her dead father's will would ensure that her considerable wealth would pass to him. However, when his plan was put into operation, the young woman's horrifying death was to have terrifying repercussions . . .